Catherine Cookson

Fenwick Houses

CORGI BOOKS
A DIVISION OF TRANSWORLD PUBLISHERS LTD

FENWICK HOUSES
A CORGI BOOK 0 552 11336 0

Originally published in Great Britain
by Macdonald & Co. (Publishers) Ltd.

PRINTING HISTORY
Macdonald edition published 1960
Corgi edition published 1970
Corgi edition reprinted 1970 (twice)
Corgi edition reprinted 1972
Corgi edition reprinted 1973 (twice)
Corgi edition reprinted 1974 (twice)
Corgi edition reprinted 1975
Corgi edition reprinted 1976
Corgi edition reprinted 1977
Corgi edition reprinted 1978
Corgi edition reprinted 1978
Corgi edition reissued 1979
Corgi edition reprinted 1980 (twice)
Corgi edition reprinted 1981

This book is set in 10 pt. Plantin

Corgi Books are published by
Transworld Publishers Ltd.,
Century House, 61–63 Uxbridge Road,
Ealing, London W5 5SA
Set, printed and bound in Great Britain by
Cox & Wyman Ltd, Reading

Catherine Cookson was born in East Jarrow and the place of her birth provides the background she so vividly creates in many of her novels. Although acclaimed as a regional writer – her novel THE ROUND TOWER won the Winifred Holtby Award for the best regional novel of 1968 – her readership spreads throughout the world. Her work has been translated into twelve languages and Corgi alone has over 20,000,000 copies of her novels in print, including those written under the name of Catherine Marchant.

Mrs Cookson was born the illegitimate daughter of a poverty-stricken woman, Kate, whom she believed to be her older sister. Catherine began work in service but eventually moved South to Hastings where she met and married a local grammar school master. At the age of forty she began writing with great success about the lives of the working class people of the North-East with whom she had grown up, including her intriguing autobiography, OUR KATE. More recently THE CINDER PATH has established her position as one of the most popular of contemporary women novelists.

Mrs Cookson now lives in Northumberland, overlooking the Tyne.

Also by Catherine Cookson

and published by Corgi Books

Fenwick Houses

CHAPTER ONE

I KEEP my eyes closed when Sam and the doctor come into
the room for they expect to find them closed, and I can think
better with them closed; think of the strange washed feeling of
my mind, for it has just been catapulted out of hell. This feeling takes some getting used to, for I have been in hell such a
long time ... twenty years, and twenty years is a lifetime any
time, but when it begins when the body is young and crying out
to live it spreads itself into an eternity.

I was just sixteen when I realized that priests don't know
everything. You don't go to hell because you sin, but because
you love; and you haven't to wait until you die, either, to meet
the Devil – oh no, he is your neighbour, I should know. Yet
should I not say rather that I lived next door to evil as distinct
from the Devil? For the Devil, poor soul, like myself isn't all
bad. He is to evil as a commissionaire is to the film showing on
the screen, someone you must pass before coming to the real
thing. .... Sixteen and twenty are thirty-six. That is my age.

'Why can't she pull round?'

That is Sam's voice, rough, kind, squeezing under the
bedclothes and patting at my body in soft, soft tones. Bringing comfort, always bringing comfort ... kind Sam, dear,
dear Sam. Sam, who is made up of love and sacrifice.

That doctor thinks he knows everything. Doctors do. He is
not even bothering to whisper. Why is he so sure that I can't
hear him?

'Well, it's up to her now, but under the circumstances
she'll likely take this way out, just slip away. She won't want
to face the battle again. Once they've been on the track she's
been on all these years, they can't turn back.'

Thank you, Doctor. Somewhere far inside me I am laughing at the doctor.

'But I would help her.' Sam's voice again, deep and eager now, its tone like a compassionate hand with pity dripping from its fingers. Oh, Sam, you make my heart sore. . . . But that doctor – Dear! dear! listen to him.

'I'm afraid, Sam, your's isn't the help that is necessary for her survival, she must find the help within herself. You know, when you feel you are no longer any use either to God or man, you give up. How long has she been in a coma this time?'

'Fifteen hours.'

'They'll likely get longer, and she'll go out in one of them.'

Thank you, Doctor, thank you, its nice to know anyway.

'Could the bullet have affected her brain, do you think, Doctor?'

'No, Sam, it went nowhere near it, and the wound healed beautifully. No, she just wants to go and nobody can stop her but herself.'

Nobody but myself . . . nobody but myself. I have the power of life and death. I am greater than Father Ellis now, greater than a priest. I can command myself 'Go' and I will go; I can say, 'No more agony, no more body longings, or bottle longings, and no shame of both.' Constance wrote, 'Shame is the fire that cleanses the soul.' She must have thought a lot about it to write that at seventeen. But her shame was one kind and mine another. My shame didn't cleanse my soul, it burnt it up; shrivelled it up like fried bacon skin. Yet once it was done I laughed again – most of the time anyway. Thank God for laughter. They used to say I had a lovely laugh. Listen. . . . Hear me? . . . There's my laugh, echoing over the fells, over the river . . . The river. If I could open my eyes I could see the river.

Well you can open them now for they're gone. Go on open them. It is daylight and the sun will be on the water. Open them and look. Don't be afraid for you can close them again and slip away at any time. Didn't he say so?

The sun is blinding, dazzling; I can see nothing but light. It hurts, but I want to see the river. . . . There, there it is, like a string of herrings, all scaly and shiny. That's how our Ronnie used to describe it when we were children and stood looking down on it from the fell. 'It's like a string of herrings,' he would say. Were we ever children? Of course, we were. Move your eyes and look there, right across the valley. Don't look at

8

the jumble of new red roofs, look past them, over Bog's End. Go on, lift your lids, look right up . . . high up. There it is, the fortress of pain wherein you were a child and you learned to laugh, only it looks nothing like a fortress, it's just a solitary little street called Fenwick Houses. Six of them, six of the ugliest, two-storey, flat-faced houses man could devise. Why did Mr. Fenwick place them up there, on such a height, with the end one pushing its nose almost into the wood? And why did he cut down the trees to give the front windows a clear view across Fellburn, right to Brampton Hill on the opposite side of the valley, and place the back windows so that they could suck in the wide expanse of sky that roofed the fells and the river?

When I'd asked this question of my dad, he had said, 'Because old man Fenwick had a spite in for people, for only beggars or blasted fools would stick out a winter in Fenwick Houses.' Yet he has stuck out forty of them, right from the day he married. And he's no fool and not quite a beggar. Well, I can give thanks for one thing . . . I was born up there, and ran out my childhood years like a wild thing in the woods and on the fells, and plodged in the river and laughed with the rock-trapped waters. If I listen hard enough I can hear myself laughing. I can see myself running down the hill to the river, our Ronnie after me, Don Dowling by his side, and Sam, fat and wobbling, coming up in the rear.

O to laugh again. To laugh. To laugh. . . .

'I can race you, I can beat you . . . whoopee!'

'Got you!' Ronnie's hand gripped my arm and wrenched me round, and I fell on my face and he fell on top of me and Don on top of him. Don's weight seemed to knock me through the earth and break all my bones and I wanted to cry, but laughed until they got up. Then I did cry, yet laughed at the same time, and Sam, seeing my tears, started to cry, too.

Sam was only three, I was five, and my brother Ronnie two years older. Don Dowling was the same age as Ronnie, and Don and Sam were brothers, and for years I thought they were my cousins and I called their mother and father Aunt and Uncle.

The Dowlings lived next door to us in number eight. We were the third house in the road, number six. On the Dowlings'

9

other side lived the Browns. They were old, really old, although Mr. Brown still went to the pit. They had two daughters who were married, and every Sunday these daughters came back to tea, and always without fail, or at least so it seemed to me then, they carried a new baby up the steep hill. I mustn't have been far wrong, because my mother said Sunday was the noisiest day of the week with the Brown squad racing around the street, for they never, like us children, made for the fells and the river. Mother said it was because they had been bred cooped up in the town and were afraid of open spaces.

Number twelve, the end house, was empty. It was often empty. On the other side of us in number four were the Pattersons. They had no children, and were funny because they were not Catholics. Everybody who wasn't a Catholic was funny. In number two, the first house, lived the Campbells. Cissie Campbell was three years older than me, and later I went to school with her. All the men in Fenwick Houses worked in the pit, and all the families were Catholics except the Pattersons, and everybody knew everything about everybody, so everybody knew that everybody feared being stood off.

When I heard the term 'stood off', I had a picture of a giant grabbing my dad by the seat of the pants and flinging him through the air to land in the roadway outside the colliery gates. Then I would see him sitting on his hunkers, his bait tin dangling between his knees, and on each side of him stretched a line of men, all sitting in the same position. To this picture I would add another. It would be that of my mother taking a heaped-up plate of dinner and standing over my dad, saying, 'There, lad, get that down you.' The sight of dad tucking away would make me happy again, and I would fling my arms about myself and jump off the floor, and everybody would laugh and say, 'There, she's at it again.'

The day our Ronnie and Don Dowling jumped on me was not the first thing I can remember. My first memory was of waking up one night and hearing Aunt Phyllis and Uncle Jim fighting next door. Their room was next to mine on the other side of the thin wall, and in later years if I strained my ears I could hear every word they said. But this night the sound of Uncle Jim's high, angry voice frightened me, and I cried out, and mother came in and gathered me into her arms. And as she marched with me out of the room, she said to Dad, as he stood in the doorway in his shirt, dusting the sleep out of his eyes, 'It's disgusting.' I was picking up words then, and for days I went around saying, 'It's dis . . . custin.'

As I grew I gathered knowledge, if unwittingly, from the rows between Aunt Phyllis and Uncle Jim.

Our house was a happy house because my mother thought of nothing but our welfare and filling our stomachs with good food. Clothes didn't matter so much. These she patched and darned and cut down and re-made. But the table did matter, and she was extravagant in this way.

Dad was of a happy, easy-going nature. He was a good two inches shorter than mother, and he adored her. I can see him now putting his arm about her waist and pulling her to him, saying, 'If you're all right, lass, there's nowt wrong in Heaven or earth.' And that was true for him. Even being stood off didn't hold the terror for Dad that it did for other men, for so great was his faith in mother that he felt she would find ways to provide for our needs. He had a saying, 'Keep it up,' and he would apply this to most things in life. To jokes until they became boring, to laughter long after it had ceased to ring true, but also to kindliness and to fantasies. Even when I was twelve I still believed in Santa Claus, for each year, as Christmas approached, he would regale us with this benevolent gentleman's kindness and generosity. Ronnie would play up to him, as we wrote letters to Dear Santa, and when our Ronnie read his out we would all double up with laughter. One such letter brought him a crack along the ear from my mother, for after asking for impossible and silly things, he finished up by saying, 'and, dear Santa, will you please put a man in Miss Spiers's stockin.' Miss Spiers was the spinster who had taken the end house, and from her first day in it it became evident that she didn't like children, particularly boys.

I knew that my Aunt Phyllis was jealous of my mother, and when I looked at them together I couldn't understand how they came to be sisters. It was years before it was explained to me that they weren't sisters at all. It had come about in this way. My grandmother died when my mother was a year old, and my grandfather married again. There were no children of this marriage. When my grandfather was killed in the pit, my mother's stepmother too married once more, and my Aunt Phyllis was born. My mother was three years older than my Aunt Phyllis, but looked ten years younger because she had a happy face. The house next door was where my mother was born, but when her stepmother died she left a will leaving all the furniture to my Aunt Phyllis. My mother was married at the time, and she told me, years later, that she hadn't minded my Aunt Phyllis getting the furniture; but I think she had, because in the first place it had all belonged to her own mother and father.

I knew from a very early age that my Aunt Phyllis loved Don and didn't love Sam. Sam was always getting smacked and pushed around, and he was put to bed without a light. And he used to raise the house and Aunt Phyllis wouldn't go up to him – she called it training. But we always knew when Uncle Jim came in, for we heard his heavy steps on the stairs, and we knew he had lifted Sam up. Then one day I saw a funny thing in Aunt Phyllis's. I dashed unannounced into her kitchen, and there she was sitting with her feet on the fender, her skirt tucked up above her knees, and in her lap was Don, and his mouth was at her bare breast. She jumped up so quickly that Don fell on to the floor. Then she went for me for not knocking and said 'Get out!' But as I was retreating through the back door she called me in again and gave me a big slice of cake. She was a good cook in the pastry line, but she was never generous with her food like my mother. And then I remember she told us both to go out on the fells, and I forgot the incident until years later.

The happiness of our house was such that at times it became unbearable. In class, when I would think of our kitchen, I could smell the bread baking and see the face of my mother as she dished out a meal. I could even smell the particular meal I was visualizing, and this would bring the saliva dripping from my mouth, and there would come over me a desire to shout and yell for joy. This being impossible, I would hug myself. But always when I hugged myself I wanted to leap from the ground, to let free a strange kind of feeling from inside of me. This feeling had nothing to do with the earth, but seemed to find its metier when I was in mid-air or when, as in dreams that came later, I flew through the air.

One night as we sat round the table eating our usual big tea, our Ronnie, gulping on a mouthful of food, looked across at my mother and said, 'Did our Christine tell you she got the cane the day?'

'No.' My mother leant towards me. 'What did you get the cane for?'

I looked down at my plate and, moving my bread around the dip, said, 'She said I was dreaming.'

'You weren't paying attention,' said my mother. 'That's your biggest fault and you've got to get over it.'

'What were you thinking, hinny?' asked my father, with a twinkle in his eye.

I returned the twinkle and said, 'Home, and this.' I pulled my nose down at my plate. Then we all threw ourselves this way and that, rocking with laughter, until my mother said, 'Now, now, get on with it.' Then she added, 'If you don't pay attention, you'll never be clever.'

Somehow I didn't care if I wasn't clever.

To share in our happiness, or rather, I think, to make it complete, there was Father Ellis. Every week, winter and summer, Father Ellis came up the hill to visit us. It was mostly on a Friday. Sometimes in the summer he would call in twice during the week, because he used to cut across Top Fell to visit Mrs. Bertram in her little farm in the next valley. But always he would have a cup of tea and a great shive of hot, lardy cake with butter on it. I always hurried home on a Friday so that I could sit close to his side and listen to him talk. Very often I couldn't understand half of what he was saying to my mother and dad, but I always got a feeling of comfort from his presence. And from looking up into his face I learned to appreciate beauty, for he had a beautiful face. He was young, and eager, and full of life, and brimming over with humour. This humour took the form of jokes, nearly always against himself or the Church, and Pat and Mick were the two figures on whom he based his kindly derision. I loved Father Ellis with a love that outshone every other affection in my life at that time, as did many an older girl. And he had a special love for me I knew, for we never met but he took my hand and said something that warmed my being.

Father Ellis never stayed so long in Aunt Phyllis's as he did in our house, and it was a sore point with her. Although she never came into the open about it she would make such statements as, 'Gallivantin' about, that's all that one does, leaving Father Howard to do the work. Talk's all he's good for!'

Then one day Uncle Jim went to the priest about Aunt Phyllis. I was about eight at the time, and I remember her coming into our kitchen. Her face drawn and grey, she stood confronting my mother, saying, 'Going to the priest! Telling the priest that, the filthy swine.' My mother had pushed me out of the door with the order to go and bring Ronnie to his tea, and that night I was woken again with the voices coming through the wall. And when about a foot from my face something crashed into the wall, I jumped out of bed and stood on the mat biting my lip, not knowing what to do. And as I stood there I heard the front room door open downstairs.

My mother and dad slept in the front room. Ronnie slept in the bedroom across the landing, and I had a tiny little room to myself. I was just going to get back into bed when I heard Aunt Phyllis's door crash closed and I went to the window and looked out. We never drew the curtains as no one could see you at the back except the birds swinging across the sky. I peered down into the yard, then over the backyard wall, and saw the dark, hunched figure of Uncle Jim striding fellwards. Then from next door came the sound of Sam crying, and this rose into a quick crescendo punctuated by the sound of slapping. Aunt Phyllis was smacking Sam's bottom. But why? Sam couldn't have done anything. He was only frightened of waking up in the dark. I found it impossible to get back into bed so went out on to the landing. Ronnie's door was closed, but from the bottom of the stairs came a gleam of light and I knew that my mother was up and had lit the lamp in the kitchen. As I crept down the stairs I heard her voice saying, 'Go after him, Bill,' and my father answering, 'No, lass it isn't a thing a man wants to talk about.' Then he said, 'Some women don't want a man. Phyllis is made that way. The only thing she ever wanted was a bairn, and just one bairn at that. She'll drive him mad. But he was wrong to go to the priest, for now she's put up the couch for him in the front room.'

As I reached the kitchen door, Sam's yelling reached even

a higher pitch, and I saw my mother strike the table with her fist as she said, 'But why has she got to take it out of the bairn?' I gave a shudder with the cold and they both swung round startled.

'What you up for, child?' demanded my mother.

'I couldn't sleep. They woke me. It was a bang against the wall. And, oh, Mam' – I stuck my finger's in my ears – 'she's still walloping Sam.'

'Come away in here and have a drink of tea.' My father gathered me into his arms and sat me on his knee before the fire, and, leaning forward, he poked the dying embers into a glow again. When my mother handed him a steaming cup of tea he did not immediately take it from her, but putting up his hand he touched her shoulder, covered with an old blue serge coat that she wore over her nightie, and never has any music held such depth of feeling or voice such sincerity as his as he murmured, 'Lass, we should go down on our bended knees and thank God that we match.'

For answer, my mother thrust the cup into his hand, saying, 'Bill! Talking like that! We've got big ears, me lad.' I knew the big ears were meant for me. 'Little pigs have big ears,' was a frequent saying of hers when she didn't want Dad to talk in front of us. Now he only smiled gently, and pouring some of the tea into his saucer he blew on it for me before I drank.

The following day I waited for Sam coming out of the Infants, and taking him by the hand I led him home. When we were half-way up the hill, Don's voice hailed us, and we stopped and waited for him. And when I wouldn't join in a race down to the river he walked behind us, chanting in a teasing voice:

> 'Sam, Sam, the dirty man,
> Washed himself in the frying pan,
> Combed his hair with a monkey's tail,
> Scratched his belly with his big-toe nail.'

I could feel Sam's hand getting stiffer and stiffer within mine. Then suddenly he tore himself from me and, swinging round, sprang on Don.

Don, even at this age, was big and stolid, and the result was that poor little Sam seemed to bounce off him. Anyway, he fell on his bottom in the middle of the road, and when I solicitously went to pick him up, he turned on me, too; then scrambling to his feet, he ran off, not towards home, but on to the fells. When I was about to follow him Don's arms went about me and pinned me to him, my back to his chest. And his voice was still laughing as he said, 'If you'll come down to the river with me I won't touch him when I get in; if you don't I'll belt him.'

I went down to the river with him. When we reached it, he decided to plodge, and with a 'Come on!' ordered me to take off my shoes and stockings.

I was nothing loath to do this for I loved plodging, but we had a special place for plodging and this wasn't it. Here the river wound round the bend, and the curve was strewn with rocks, which if you were agile enough you could use as stepping stones, but beyond the rocks the water tumbled and frothed. It was too deep for plodging. When Ronnie stood in this part it came up to his shoulders, so when Don, gripping my hand, pulled me on to the stepping stones, I cried, 'Eeh! no, Don . . . not down there! It's too deep.'

Although I had played by the river since I had played at all, I was still unable to swim. The reason for this was simple; my mother had forbidden me to go into the water with the boys other than for a plodge. Sometimes when they swam I would stand on the bank yelling and laughing and shouting at them as they dived and plunged and larked about. Even Sam at six could swim, and for a bathing costume he had a pair of little white pants that kept slipping down and which were sometimes pulled down purposely by Don who would pretend it was just – carrying on.

I had strict orders from my mother that I was never to go into the water with the boys, and that if they went up to Pollard's burn I hadn't to go with them at all. I knew that this was because a lot of boys gathered at Pollard's burn at the week-end and swam with nothing on. But now Don was pulling me towards the deep water and I screamed at him to stop, for already the bottom of my dress and knickers were wet, and the water, spurting from between the stones, was stinging my legs like pins and needles.

My arms about his waist I cried, 'Don! Don! Let me go back.'

He stood perfectly still in the water, and looking down at me, he said, 'Well, if I do, will you promise never to wait for our Sam any more?'

'Yes . . . yes, I promise, Don.' I would have promised anything to get out of that swirling water.

'Swear.'

'I swear, Don.'

'Cross your heart.'

I released one trembling arm and religiously crossed my heart somewhere in the region of my collar bone. But now, having given him the assurance that he wanted, he did not let me go back towards the bank but, his face becoming stiff, he said, 'You heard me mum and dad row last night, didn't you?'

I looked at him and nodded once.

'It's none of your business.' He grabbed me roughly by the shoulder.

'No, Don,' I said, 'no, it isn't.'

'I'd like to shoot me dad . . . string him up.'

'Don!' My horror and amazement made me forget my fear for the moment, and I gasped, 'I like your dad, he's nice.'

'You!'

Petrified, I felt myself being pressed backwards and was on the point of screaming when our Ronnie's voice, coming from the bank, shouting, 'What you think you're up to? Let her go!' surprised Don so much that he did let me go, and I overbalanced and, yelling my head off, fell on my back into the water.

I hadn't time to go under before Don's hands gripped me, and, pulling me upwards, he dragged me to the bank, where Ronnie, already in the water, demanded angrily, 'What you think you're up to, eh? Frightenin' her!'

'I wasn't frightenin' her, we was just playin'.'

'Playin'! She was cryin' . . . scared.' He turned his head towards me. 'Weren't you?'

I gulped, but did not answer him. Instead, I said, 'Me mam'll pay me . . . look at me pinny!'

They neither of them looked at my pinny but stood staring at each other. They were both of about the same height, only Ronnie wasn't half as thick as Don. The next moment they were rolling on the ground, punching and using their knees in each other's stomachs.

'Give over! Give over!' I yelled at them. 'Oh, give over!' And when they didn't I turned and ran, and never stopped until I reached the kitchen, there to cry out that our Ronnie and Don were fighting.

But my mother took no notice of this, only of my wet state. And stripping me, she said, 'You'll go to bed without any tea for this.'

Then the river and the fight were forgotten. Even sending me to bed was forgotten, for my dad came in, and from the first sight of his face my mother knew what he was about to tell her.

She stood at one side of the kitchen table and he at the other, and, putting his bait tin slowly and definitely down and speaking to it, he said, 'I wonder if it'll be the last time I'll use thee, lad?'

I saw my mother swallow twice before she said, 'How many?'

'Over a hundred,' he replied.

My mother's eyes moved down to the table, across it, then came to rest on the bait tin, on which my dad still had his hands. Then throwing up her head and putting her hands behind her back to adjust the strings of a fancy little apron, which she had made herself out of the skirt of a summer frock and which she usually wore from a Friday tea-time until Sunday night, she exclaimed, 'Well, and now we know. So we can get on with it.'

And as she went about, putting the water into the big tin bath that stood before the fire, she talked of her plans for the future as if they had been long arranged in her mind. 'You can apply for a bit of that land at the wood edge for an allotment. That'll keep us going for veg, anyway.'

I watched her disappear into the scullery and heard the bucket being dipped into the washhouse pot, and as she poured the steaming water into the bath she announced, 'And I'll go back to Mrs. Durrant's.'

'Will you, lass?'

My dad had already divested himself of all his clothes except his short pants.

'Yes. She said that if I ever wanted work I had just to go and tell her.'

My mother had been in service at Mrs. Durrant's on Brampton Hill before she was married, and although she had left the place over eight years now, there still occasionally came a parcel of clothing from her late mistress.

My father stepped into the water and began to soap himself, and when the time came for my mother to wash his back, she said, comfortingly, 'Don't worry. We've still got our breath and a bit of spunk left.'

She had hardly finished speaking when the door opened and my Aunt Phyllis came in. Seeing my father in the bath she turned her eyes away from him, and her voice coming in rapid jerks she addressed my mother, who was once more at the table.

'What we goin' to do? This is the end. They'll never start again. It's only an excuse to shut the pit down. It's old.'

My mother turned to the oven and, taking a big, steaming earthenware dish from the shelf, said, as she passed my father, 'Watch yourself, lad,' and she placed the dish in the middle of the table before answering my Aunt Phyllis. Then deliberately she turned and, making a motion of drying her hands on the hessian oven cloth, she said quietly, 'We'll all have to do the best we can then.'

'And what's that? . . . starve?'

'We needn't starve, we've got our hands. There'll be some kind of work for women.'

'You'll go to Mrs. Durrant's, I suppose. Well, I can't see meself going skivvying for anybody, and what's more I'm not going to either.'

'That's your business.' My mother still went on quietly with the drying motion, and there was a silence in the kitchen except for the plodging noise my father was now making in the water. Then my Aunt Phyllis said in thin, steel-like tones,

'He'll get hissel' away and find work, there's other towns besides this, there's bound to be work some place.'

My father now turned his head over his shoulder and, looking at my Aunt Phyllis asked, 'You thinking about going with him, Phyllis, then?'

For answer my Aunt Phyllis gave him one long look, before

turning on her heel and going out, slamming the door after her....

My mother went to Mrs. Durrant and got three mornings' work a week. My father did as she bade him and took a piece of ground on the outskirts of the woods, and we had always plenty of taties and things, with the result that our table remained the same. The smells of cooking perfumed the house, and nothing was changed for at least three years, except that we couldn't send our shoes to the cobblers and my dad did them and the nails stuck through and tore my stockings.

But there were more men lining the bridge at the bottom of the hill where it crossed the river. Some sat on top of the wall, some sat on their hunkers with their backs to the wall, some dangled sticks with string on and played at catching fish, and some did catch fish, but on the sly, for they would get something if they were caught fishing without a licence in the river.

For coal my father went to the tip and brought back bags of slack, and at first my mother had her work cut out on baking days, until she got the idea of wetting the slack and putting it into tins. It fell to our Ronnie and me to gather the tins.

Next door they did not fare so well. Although my Uncle Jim had come in with Dad in the allotment, his heart was never in the work, and I heard my dad say he dug as if he was using a spoon at a tea party. This was odd because I also heard Dad say that there wasn't a better hewer in the pit than my Uncle Jim.

Hardly a day went by but my mother set up Don and Sam to a meal, and so they became to me like our family, until one day this procedure was brought to an abrupt stop.

There had been a lot of talk of late between my mother and Aunt Phyllis about Don, doctors, and hospitals. It was all very mysterious until one evening Don joined us by the river. We knew Aunt Phyllis had taken him to the doctor's because Sam had told us. Sam, Ronnie and I were at our usual pastime, they at swimming and I at plodging. Don hailed us as he came running down the hill, and when he stood on the edge of the bank he could hardly speak for lack of wind and excitement, and when we gathered round him he told us excitedly that he was going into hospital. 'And you know what?' he said. We

20

waited in silence, our eyes fixed on him, 'I'm going to be split up, there and there.' He made two clipping movements with his forefinger up his groins, and when my face screwed up in horror, he said, 'That long.' His fingers on his groins measured about nine inches, and I felt my stomach heaving in horror at the thought of what he would have to endure.

That night I said to my mother, 'Poor Don is going to be cut up, Mam,' and she said, 'Nonsense. Who told you that?'

'He did.'

She went away mumbling, yet I thought I made out what she was saying. Yet I knew that I couldn't have heard aright, for what I imagined she said was, 'Good thing if he was.'

Don went to hospital, and after a few days he returned, covered in glory. Somehow it had been very nice while Don was away, because Sam was different. He talked more, laughed more, he had even told a Pat and Mick joke at the table, and my mother choked on her food as much in surprise at Sam telling a joke as at the joke itself. But once Don came back Sam was quiet again.

On the afternoon he returned we made an expedition, not to the river, but into the wood to gather blackies, for it was blackberry time and my mother wanted to make as much jelly as she could. But we were some time getting started on our picking for we were all listening open-mouthed to Don's description of the hospital and the things that had happened to him there. He got so excited in relating what had taken place that nothing would stop him from illustrating it, and when he lay down and started to perform an imaginary operation on himself, Ronnie threw cold water on the whole proceedings by saying, 'Oh, get up man, and don't be so daft, you would have been dead if they had done that!'

Don got up and without further words we started our picking, but I sensed that he was huffed at our Ronnie not believing him, and I felt sorry for him. I didn't like it when people didn't believe me, and didn't laugh when I told a funny joke. It made me feel silly, and I knew that was how Don was feeling. So I started picking near him, and when quite close I whispered, 'I believe you, Don.' He looked at me, then taking my hand pulled me away round the bushes, and there he whispered, 'Do you?'

I nodded, then emphasized, 'Yes, I do.'

My hand was still in his and quietly he drew me away until we were in a tangle of blackberry bushes, and then he whispered, 'Look, lie down and I'll show you what they did to me.'

'Me?' I said. 'Lie down?'

'Yes, I'll show you what they did to me in the hospital.'

He pressed hard down on my shoulders and I shrank away from him, saying, 'No, no, I'm not going to lie down. I believe you, but I'm not going to lie down.'

There was a look on his face that filled me with a sort of jerky fright. My stomach was reacting as if I was receiving a succession of shocks, it was jumping within me.

'Lie down.'

'Not, I'll not.'

'You will, I'll make you.'

'I'll shout for our Ronnie.'

His eyes darted to the height of the bushes, then with a fierce thrust he knocked me backwards and the next minute I was yelling with the pain of the brambles as they seemed to pierce every part of my body.

It was Sam who reached me first and pulled me up, then our Ronnie, coming on the scene, said, 'You would fall into something. And where's the blackies?'

The few blackberries that I had in my can were lost among the brambles now, and I began to cry.

'All right, all right, don't bubble. Come on.'

Ronnie's words were tender. Ronnie was nearly always tender with me, like I was with Sam. The three of us together were joined with a harmonious thread, but Don was the needle through which the thread was drawn, and its point was vicious, and I was to learn within the next few hours just how vicious.

We were sitting in the kitchen, my mother, Dad and myself, when I heard my Aunt Phyllis come into the scullery. I knew it was her before I saw her for she always rattled the back-door latch.

When she stood at the kitchen door we all knew something was wrong, for her thin lips lay tight upon one another and had caused a little puff of flesh at each side of her mouth, as if she was in the act of blowing up a balloon.

'I want a word with you, Annie.'

My mother looked at me, then said, 'It's about your bed-time.'

'I haven't washed, Mam.' I was looking at my Aunt Phyllis.

'Oh, well then, go and have your wash now.'

I went past Aunt Phyllis as she stood in the scullery door-way and something seemed to fall from her face, something hard and malevolent, and it pressed on me and drove my eyes away from hers towards the floor.

The clean water bucket in the scullery was empty, so I took it down to the bottom of the yard and put it under the tap, then turned the tap slowly on. For some reason or other I didn't want to return too quickly to the house, the reason was mixed up with my Aunt Phyllis's look. When the pail was full to the top and I knew that I would have to empty some out before I could carry it up the yard, my mother's voice came sharp and harsh from the doorway, crying, 'Christine!'

I walked slowly up the yard. My mother was waiting for me at the back door, and she looked at me steadily for a moment before her hand dropped to my shoulder, and without a word she guided me into the kitchen. My dad was standing on the mat and my Aunt Phyllis near the table, and when my mother led me into the room she turned me so that I faced my Aunt Phyllis. Then she said, calmly, 'What were you doing in the woods this afternoon?'

I lifted my eyes to hers without moving my head, and said, 'You know, Mam, getting blackberries.'

'What else did you do? Did you play with Don?'

'Play with Don?'

'Yes, that's what I said, play with Don.'

I looked at her and considered. Could what had happened behind the bushes be considered as play? I didn't think that it could, and I said, 'No, Mam.'

I heard the air being taken up through my mother's nose, and in the beam of the fading sun that slanted into the kitchen my whole attention became riveted on the golden hairs that quivered on the inside of her broad nostrils. I had never noticed before that she had hairs on the inside of her nose. She jerked my thoughts back to the matter in hand by saying, sharply, 'Christine, pay attention!'

'Yes, Mam.'

'What were you doing in the woods this afternoon?'

'Only pickin'—'

'You know you weren't, you were doing bad things ... naughty things!' Now Aunt Phyllis was leaning over me, and her face looked dirty, as if it hadn't been washed for a long time. But my Aunt Phyllis was always washing herself and doing her hair. I stepped back away from her face, and said, 'Eeh, no, I wasn't! I never ... I don't!'

It was Dad's hand that steadied me. Sitting down he called me to order.

'Now, hinny, don't worry, you've only got to tell the truth. I promise you you won't get into trouble, you won't get your backside smacked.'

There was no laughter in my dad's eyes nor in any other part of his face, and this, like a douche of cold water, brought it startlingly home to me that the matter was serious, very serious. If my dad wasn't laughing with any part of his face there was something very wrong. So I turned from him and, looking at my mother, I said, 'I never done anything naughty, Mam. Don took me behind the bushes. He wanted me to lie down so he could show me about the operation, and I wouldn't. ...'

I felt my dad's fingers pressing on my hands, and when I looked back at him he was looking across the room to my Aunt Phyllis, and he said quietly, 'What do you say to that, Phyllis?'

'I say she's a little liar.'

'Well, it's up to us to say the same about Don, isn't it?'

'Look, I know my Don, he wouldn't have come home in that state if he had been telling a lie. He was upset, I've never seen the lad so upset, disgusted I would say. Surprised and disgusted at her. You've always given her too much rope ... running mad about the fells like a wild thing.'

'That's our business, Phyllis, how we bring up our bairns.' It was my mother speaking, her voice tight and steady. 'And I'm telling you here and now that I don't believe a word of it. If you had said it was Cissie Campbell I might have believed you, but—'

'But not when it's her, oh, no!' Aunt Phyllis's tone was deriding. 'Well, let me tell you, if she was to go down on her bended knees before a priest this minute and tell him that she didn't do it, I wouldn't believe her, so there. And that's my last word on the matter.' She turned her gaze on me again, then most surprisingly she said, her voice laden with bitterness, 'You and your silly laugh.'

The kitchen door and the back door had banged before any of us moved, then my mother with her fingers linked tightly together came to me and, kneeling down so that her face was on a level with mine and my dad's, she said to me softly, 'Christine, pay attention. . . . Tell me, did you . . .? Now don't be frightened, just tell me if you did or not. . . . Did you take your . . . your knickers off when Don was there and . . . and . . .' Before she had finished her struggling words I cried, 'No! Mam, no! You know I wouldn't do that.' Her hand covered mine when it was resting on my dad's knee, and she said, still quietly, 'I thought you wouldn't.'

My mother got to her feet and went and looked out of the window, and after a few moments she said, 'This is going to make things awkward.'

'Aye,' said Dad, 'it will for a time, but it'll pass over. Lads get funny notions; he's at a funny age. Try to think of that, Annie.'

My mother still kept looking out of the window as she said, 'I've never liked Don, and now I know why.'

Dad made a sound that wasn't a laugh but tried to be as he said, 'Well, she's returned the compliment: she doesn't like ours.'

He didn't say which one of us my Aunt Phyllis disliked, but the pressure on my arm as he automatically pulled me nearer told me. And I remember the surprise I felt, for whenever I went into the house next door I was always nice to my Aunt Phyllis. I had never answered her back, not once, and I had never been cheeky to her – oh no, that was the last thing I would have dreamed of – and I always noticed when she had something new and would say, 'I like that, Aunt Phyllis,' although very often I didn't know what the things were for. And when I would go in to my mother and say excitedly, 'Aunt Phyllis has got a new tablecloth, Mam, silky it is,' or, 'Aunt Phyllis has a new ornament, Mam,' she would make no comment whatever, but always tell me to get on with this or that, or go out to play. And because of my mother's attitude I felt that I was the only one who noticed my Aunt Phyllis's nice things, so besides being surprised I felt hurt to know that she didn't like me.

But even all this upset was obliterated from my mind the next day when Fitty Gunthorpe was thrust on to my horizon. Fitty lived in a caravan with his father on a piece of spare ground at the edge of Bog's End. He was a man six foot or more tall, thin and gangling and subject to epileptic fits. He was known to everybody as Fitty Gunthorpe, but he was also known to be quite harmless and very fond of animals. At times I had met him in the wood, and he aroused no fear in me. He had a little dog forever at his heels – they said the dog was never parted from him night or day. It was the sight of the dog that inspired the wish in me to have one of my own, and I had mentioned this to my father and had received a vague promise of 'Aye, I'll look out for one.' But it wasn't the dog but a rabbit that brought Fitty Gunthorpe into my life.

I was never one for lying in bed in the mornings. Often I was out of bed and had been down to the river, just to have a look, while my mother was getting the breakfast ready, and was back in the house before Ronnie stumbled downstairs, his knuckles in his eyes and his mouth agape. And when I would say to him, 'Oh, Ronnie, the river's lovely this morning,' he would reply, 'Oh, you, you're barmy, up all night.'

Some mornings I went into the fields or the wood to pick flowers to take to my teacher. There was always something to be picked at different times of the year, cowslips – not buttercups or daisies, they were too common – catkins, wood anemones, ferns, bluebells and may, beautiful scented white may.

This particular morning was bright golden, and soft and warm, and the birds were all singing. I could distinguish some of them by their song: the lark, of course, for its voice shot it into the heavens, and I could tell the difference between the thrush, the blackbird, and the robin. But this morning I did not run up the street or hug myself and leap from the ground at the sound of the bird song as I sometimes did, but went into the wood and made my way to the place where yesterday I had been with Don, for it seemed to me that I would find something there that would bear out that I had spoken the truth, and then my Aunt Phyllis would believe me. But the only evidence that I found was three blackberries lying close together on a clear piece of sward. They were laden with dew and were sparkling like jewels. They should have been able to prove in some way that Don pushed me into the bushes and upset my can, but I knew that they couldn't, and I turned away on to the path. And there I saw Fitty Gunthorpe. He came up to me, his mouth agape and smiling a welcome. The dog was at his heels. He wore no hat, and his hair was longish and brown and wavy like a girl's. It did not seem part of him, but looked like a wig.

'Ha . . . hallo,' he said.

'Hallo,' I said.

'Lo . . . lovely m . . . morning.'

And I smiled at him and said, 'Yes, it is.'

The dog took no notice of me, and they both passed by, taking the path by which I had entered the wood. This was the lower path. It started above the last house in our street and if you kept to it you would come out on the hill that looked down on to Bog's End and the spare piece of ground where the caravans were. I did not want to go that way this morning so I took a side track which led to the upper path. I think we children had made many of the tracks in the wood, and we knew them as well as we did our own backyards. The wood itself was a continuation of the hill on which Fenwick Houses stood, and the hill was tree-studded to its summit and way down the other side, too. The upper path ran in a zigzag fashion towards the top of the hill. In parts the trees were sparse, and where they let in the light the grass grew and rabbits sported. We called these various open spaces bays. There was the little bay, the big bay and the tree bay. The tree bay was my favourite, for it was the smallest sward of grass and was set in a complete circle of trees, not in rigid formation, but nevertheless enclosing the space in a rough ring. It was an enchanted place to me, and I liked it best when I could come here on my own. When I was with the lads we were never quiet.

I had to cross the second path to get to the tree bay, and it was when I reached the path that I heard the cry. It was small, a squeaking, intermittent yet linked in a continuous, pitying yelp. I scrambled over a bank of rich moss, bright green and close woven, then through the trees and to the bay. I knew the cry was that of a rabbit, and before I saw it I was already shivering with pity. The men, to supplement their tables, were catching rabbits, setting traps for them. They would set them at night and come early in the morning to clear them. I'd never seen the traps but I knew, from listening to Dad, all about them. But I understood that they were mostly set around the perimeter of the wood, for the rabbits came out to feed in the fields. This was the heart of the wood and somebody must have set a trap here. Then I saw the poor creature, and the sight riveted me to the spot. I could feel my hands coming slowly up to my mouth to still the scream. The rabbit was not struggling against the weight of a trap, but against the weight of a tree, a big tree, for one of its back legs was nailed to it. I hid my face, then I knew I was running, and thought I was running away through the wood again, and seemed surprised when I felt the rabbit's quivering body under my hands. The leg was all torn and bleeding, and when I pulled madly at the nail and the poor thing squealed loudly I began to moan. The sound reminded me of a man who had been knocked down by a car in the market last year. They had lain him in a shop doorway and he made moaning sounds. The next thing I remember was that I was running through the wood finding my way more by instinct than by sight, for I was blinded with a flood of tears. When I came out of the dimness of the wood and into the morning sunlight on the street I tore to the house, and there pushed everything before me, doors, chairs, little obstacles, and flung myself, not on my mother, but on my dad, crying, 'Dad! Dad! Come on. The poor rabbit, the poor thing. Oh, Dad . . . Dad.'

I had knocked some fried bread out of his hand and the grease had gone across the tablecloth, and my mother exclaimed, 'What on earth's up with you, child? Look what you've done. What's the matter?' Then as if attacked by a thought that had suddenly frightened her, she pulled me from my dad and, shaking me, said, 'Stop it! Stop it! What's happened?'

'A rabbit, a rabbit, a poor rabbit!' I gulped and swallowed and choked before I could voice the horror that I had seen. 'Nailed, somebody's nailed it to the tree. It's back leg, and the blood all over it.' I turned up my palms to show the blood, and Dad, who was now on his feet, said, 'Where?'

'In the bay, Dad, up at the top.'

Stopping only to put his coat on, for nothing would have induced him to go outside the door without his coat, he hurriedly followed me into the street. I ran on ahead all the way, but when we reached the bay he was only a few steps behind. Now it was he who went ahead, and then, slowly, I approached his back, he ordered me sharply, 'Stay where you are!'

I saw his arm moving in a pumping motion, but he did not fall back with the nail in his hands as I had expected. Then I saw him grope in his pocket and bring out his knife. He paused with it in his hand, then called sharply, 'Christine! go away, go away into the trees.' I turned and, putting my fingers to my ears, ran to the end of the bay.

It was not long before I heard him behind me, the rabbit was in his hands, it was dead. There was blood on its neck and it had only three legs. I fell flat on the ground and pushed my face into the wet grass, then my stomach seemed to rise through my backbone. I felt my spine drawn up in a curve, something like the hump of a fell, and then it seemed that my whole stomach came through my mouth.

I didn't go to school that day.

It was my mother's morning for Mrs. Durrant and she took me with her, and when we reached the bridge at the bottom of the hill, it seemed to be blocked by men. They weren't sitting on their hunkers or leaning over the parapet, but they were gathered together in a group. We had reached them before I realized they were listening to my dad, and it was the first time I had heard him swear. I couldn't see his face now, but I knew by his voice that it would be long and hard, for he was crying, 'If I could find the bugger who did this, I'd nail him to the bloody tree with me own hands. The bloody sod! What it's done to my Christine remains to be seen.'

I was aware of two things at this moment, my dad was using bad language and my mother was doing nothing to stop him. We rounded the circle of men as if they were all unknown to us, even the man in the centre. Some moved to make way for my mother, and as we went towards the hump on the bridge, I heard one man explain angrily, 'Let's go and find Gunthorpe,' and I had a picture of Fitty's face with the morning light on it, saying, 'Hallo.' I could see the dog close pressed against his boot and ragged trouser leg, and I was filled with a feeling which I can put no name to, just that it was a sort of sorrowful bewilderment. Fitty had always appeared a part of the wood to me, he was as natural to the wood as were the trees, yet he had nailed a rabbit to one of them; at least I had said so.

I felt so upset that the beauty and elegance of Mrs. Durrant's house was lost on me. I could not see it because I was all the time seeing a rabbit with pain-glazed eyes.

Mrs. Durrant herself came into the kitchen, and as she bent over me to stroke my hair she smelled nice. And with her hand on my head she turned to my mother and said, 'How lucky you are, Ann.' Then looking again at me, she added, 'You can't tell if it's gold or silver, I have never seen anything like it.'

As Mrs. Durrant went out she paused by my mother and asked with a laugh, 'What will you take for her?' My mother answered with another laugh, 'not all the tea in China, Ma'am.'

Mrs. Durrant had no children, but she had a lot of money and a big house and nice clothes, and that day my mother brought a big parcel back home, and a basket of food, but I couldn't be happy about either the parcel or the food.

When we got back at half-past one there was a man standing at the door, and he took off his cap when he spoke to my mother.

'You Mrs. Winter, ma'am?'

'Yes,' said my mother. 'What is it?'

'I'm John Gunthorpe.'

'Oh!' said my mother. 'Will you come in?'

He was tall like Fitty, and his hair was thick, but it was very white. His face and hands were clean, with a scrubbed look, and though his clothes were old and there was a patch on his coat pocket, there was a cleanness about them, too.

'It is your husband I want to see, missis,' he said.

'He should be in at any time. Will you have a cup of tea? I am just going to make one. It's hot work coming up the hill.'

'No, thank you, missis,' he said. He moved from one foot to the other, twisted his cap into a roll and stuck it under his oxter and looked at my mother, and she at him. Then he burst out, 'The child was mistaken, Mick wouldn't do a thing like that. He loves animals . . . he's crazy about them. He lives for nothing else.' He poked out his head at her. 'He's not an imbecile, ma'am. He has fits but he's not an imbecile.'

'No,' said my mother.

'If it weren't for his fits you know what he would have been?'

My mother said nothing, and he went on, 'A vet, that's what he would have been. And then to say that he did that, nail a rabbit to a tree.' He shook his head slowly. 'And that lot of ignorant, big-mouthed louts comin' storming to me van. They would have lynched him, missis. Do you know that? Just another spark and they would have lynched him. They've got time on their hands, nowt to do.'

I was staring at him transfixed when he came to me and, bending his long length over me, said softly, 'Me bairn, my lad didn't hurt the rabbit, try to believe that. Somebody did, some cruel man but not my lad, will you try to believe that hinny?'

I moved my head once slowly in answer, then I watched him straighten up again and say to my mother, 'Where will I find him, missus – your man?'

'He'll be on his allotment, or you'll likely meet him coming back up the hill at this time.'

'Thanks, missis, I'm obliged.'

He jerked his head at my mother, then looked at me once more, and his look was kind, so kind that I wanted to cry. And I did cry, I cried on and off all day. And when I was in bed that night I was sick and my mother had to come and clean me up.

CHAPTER TWO

THE days moved on and the rules and formulae on which childhood is based formed a skin that covered up the scar on my mind made by the rabbit. This in turn had overshadowed Don Dowling's lying, at least for me, yet I could not help but notice that the incident was still to the fore in my mother's mind, and also in Aunt Phyllis's, for they did not speak. My Uncle Jim and Dad still worked together on the allotment and there was no rift between them. I still went up into the wood and down to the river, always now accompanied by Ronnie, or by Sam when he could get out. But I did not jump or hug myself as I used to, in fact, I did not feel joy again until Christmas Eve. And then the sight of Dad putting up the coloured chains across the ceiling, and of my mother taking out of the box in which they were replaced each New Year the fragile glass swans and balls made of coloured glass brought the leaping feeling back again, and forgotten magic from past Christmases rushed at me and I flung my arms about myself and leapt in the air.

Dad was standing on a chair tying the last coloured fan in the chain to the picture rail. Mam was on her knees, kneading dough in a great earthenware dish, the one she used for double bakings. They both stopped what they were doing, looked at me as I stood laughing at them, then looked at each other, and they, too, laughed. Then my mother said a funny thing. 'The time has come,' she said, 'to end this. I must go into Phyllis.'

'Aye, lass, that's right. Good will and peace to all men.'

The kitchen was filled with such warm happiness that I only had to put my hand out to touch it. I felt I could scoop it up in handfuls from the air. I knew that I was drawing it down into my chest with long sniffs up my nose. At last I lay on the mat, my bent arms coupling my head, and stared through the little brass rods that supported the steel top of the fender, the fender that I had cleaned that morning with whiting and ashes, at the white-heated bars, behind which the fire glowed a steady, fierce red. I wasn't thinking, I wasn't even breathing, or so it seemed for I was so still. I was only feeling . . . feeling comfort. And when a child feels comfort, it feels security, and with security, love. And I had so much security that I was swimming in love.

It was some time later. I was still lying on the mat, but on my back now, looking up into the ceiling of entwined colour, because now my view of the fire had been obscured by the loaf tins my mother had placed on the fender before she had gone next door to make it up with Aunt Phyllis. But she was not gone more than a few minutes before she was back again. She came in the front way, through the front room and into the kitchen, pulling her coat from around her shoulders as she did so, and making straight for the scullery, and on her way she said to my dad, 'Here, I want you a minute.' Her tone roused me from my dreaming, and I sat up and watched Dad follow her.

'She's near mad,' I heard my mother say. Then her voice fell and became a mumble. But Dad's voice was loud as he replied. 'Well don't say she hasn't asked for it, lass. To my mind it's long overdue, and I have an idea who the woman is an' all.'

'Sh! sh!'

The kitchen door was pulled close and I turned my gaze to the fire again. The bread had risen well up over the tins, and the paste of one of the loaves was drying and cracking, and so, taking a clean tea-towel and a piece of cloth I covered the bread over, and when some minutes later my mother came from the scullery she applauded my action and gave me a pat on the head as she said airily, 'You're learning, hinny.' Then she added, 'How would you like Sam and Don to come in with us the morrow?'

She had placed Sam first, and it was only of Sam I thought as I answered, 'Oh! yes, that would be lovely, Mam. . . . For dinner and tea?'

'Yes, all day. And the morrow night we'll have a bit of jollification.'

'Oh, Mam.' I flung my arms round her waist and drew into myself more happiness. It was Christmas, and tomorrow poor little Sam would be in our kitchen all day and I would make him eat everything and see that he laughed. I did not give a thought to my Aunt Phyllis and her trouble.

The rift was closed between my mother and Aunt Phyllis, but a rift that was never to close opened between Aunt Phyllis and my Uncle Jim, and as the months built up into years the rift widened. My Uncle Jim, I gleaned, had a woman in Bog's End, yet he still continued to live next door. Whenever he earned an odd shilling or two above the dole or beyond the means test he would throw the money on the table and my Aunt Phyllis would pick it up, and they never spoke.

The woman in Bog's End kept a little shop and, out of curiosity one day, I went in and bought some sweets. She was just the opposite of Aunt Phyllis, being round and fat with a happy face, and she spoke to me nice and put an extra sweet in the bag. I liked her, and when I came out I wished Aunt Phyllis would die, so that my Uncle Jim could marry her and Sam could have a nice mam.

Sam spent more time in our house that he did in his own, and Aunt Phyllis didn't mind. But if Don came in and Aunt Phyllis heard him through the kitchen wall she would call him to fetch water or wood, or just to come into the house.

I was about eleven when Cissie Campbell drew to my notice something that should have been evident before. 'You can't move a step without them lads,' she said. Perhaps this was jealousy on Cissie's part, for neither Ronnie nor Don would have anything to do with Cissie, and Sam was too young for her notice. But her words set me thinking, although I remember that, as usual when confronted by the smallest problem, I wanted to shelve it. Yet I did give this statement some thought, for as far as I could ever work myself up into a state of annoyance, I was annoyed, and by the fact that I seemed always to have to walk in the middle of a triangle, with one of them at each corner, Ronnie, Don and Sam. Going to school, coming back, running down to the river, darting through the wood, they were there. I knew why our Ronnie was always with me, for I heard my mother saying to him one night, 'You must never leave her alone with the lads, you hear? Now understand what I am saying to you. Never leave her alone.' And he had said, 'Yes, Mam.'

My mother had said 'Lads', but I knew that she just meant Don, for she would leave Sam and me together in our kitchen while she slipped down into the town. But she would never leave me alone with Don.

From the time I became aware of this pressure around me I had a desire to thrust my way out, but the desire had no strength and, as in other things, in this I took the line of least resistance.

It was when Ronnie was thirteen that he began to argue. He had always been a great talker, but as Dad said he never knew when to stop. At this age his talking became aggressive, and he became restless, chafing at the days until he could leave school and perhaps get set on, above ground, at the Venus pit, which, even while it was standing off older men, was still setting on young ones.

It was about this time that he started a funny game. We had an old dictionary and he would open it at any page, and with the aid of a pin and closed eyes choose a word. Then he would start talking about the word and telling Dad all he knew about it, and Dad would try to keep his face straight. Sometimes he went to the library and came back with thick books, which he would throw with a clatter on the table. Many of the books he never read, not even the first page, for the subjects were as foreign to him as would have been books in French or German. There was one word though that the pin picked out which really did catch his attention, and he did read the book that he got from the library on this subject, although when my dad picked the book up he laughed and exclaimed. 'My God, he's not going to tell me he understands this.' The subject was evolution, and in some measure Ronnie did understand it, and one day he brought forth my awful admiration even while I was astounded at his temerity of daring to argue with the priest.

It was Friday tea-time, and Father Ellis was on his weekly visit, and work or no work my mother still greeted him with the slab of lardy cake, although the week after my father came out he admonished her saying, 'No, no. Now we'll have no more of this . . . a cup of tea and that is all.'

My mother had spoken to him in the same tone she used

35

to us, as if he wasn't a priest at all. 'Get it down you,' she said, 'and let it stop your noise.' He had laughed and got it down him.

My dad liked Father Ellis although he was often chided by him for not going to mass on a Sunday; he wouldn't take the excuse that his clothes weren't decent enough. I heard Dad comment on Father Ellis one day, saying, 'He's a priest as God and meself would have them.' This linking of himself to God added to my father's importance in my eyes and gave Father Ellis the prestige usually allocated to angels. And here we were this Friday, all of us around the table, and we were listening not so much to Father Ellis as to our Ronnie.

He had brought my mother's mouth agape by saying flatly there was no such thing as the Garden of Eden; he had brought my eyes popping by talking about chimpanzees and orang-outangs and gorillas. At one point he became embarrassed, but recovered himself and went on, grimly this time, about ape men and prehistoric men, whatever they were. My father's face was straight, but his eyes were alive with laughter and I knew he was finding difficulty in suppressing it. Father Ellis's face was serious, and he looked deeply impressed as if he was drinking in every word that fell from Ronnie's lips, and when finally and quite abruptly Ronnie stopped and dug his thumb into the palm of his hand as if making a full-stop to his oration, the priest nodded thoughtfully at him and said in a deeply serious tone, with not a hint of laughter in it, 'You're right, you're right.' Ronnie came back, bumptious and arrogant: 'Yes, I know I'm right, Father, and them what doesn't believe in evolution are ignorant.'

He cast a defiant yet scared glance around the table, but nobody spoke except the priest, and he said, 'Well I for one believe in evolution, quite firmly. Now look, let's get it down to ordinary level and ordinary meaning. For instance, take Mrs. McKenna, you know; her who sings above everybody in church.'

All our faces answered this with a smile, and Father Ellis followed the smile from one to the other and brought us all into this discussion by saying, 'Now you're a sensible family, there's not a more sensible one. Now ask yourselves, would the good God have made Mrs. McKenna just as she is, feet, hands and all? No, when he first made her she was as bonnie a thing as ever stepped out of Paradise, but evolution has done this to her. She's got worse and worse until she is, as you know, a bit out of the ordinary, God help her. Now mind, I'm not blaming her and don't any one of you speak a word of what I've said, do you hear me? But I'm just using her as an illustration. She is a good woman, God bless her, although she has a voice like a corn crake.'

We all tittered, all except Ronnie. He sat there, straight of face, and there was a deep furrow between his brows, and he screwed in his chair before leaning towards Father Ellis and saying sharply, 'It's no use, Father, turning it funny and going on about Mrs. McKenna, she's no illustration. We all likely started like Mrs. McKenna and—'

'Ronnie, be quiet!'

It was my mother now, brought out of her bemusement at the talking on such a thing as evolution and horrified that a son of hers should speak so to a priest. She could use any tone she liked to Father Ellis, but then she was grown-up.

'And don't you dare interrupt the Father,' she cried. 'Name of goodness, what is things coming to?'

Ronnie's lids were blinking now and his tone was much more modified as he put in, 'But I read it, Mam, it's all in my book. And it's true, I know it's true.'

'Take that!'

It wasn't a hard slap, it was just a reproving slap across the ear, but it brought Ronnie quickly to his feet. He stood for a moment looking ashamed, and Mam's hands went out to him apologetically, but he brushed them aside and went into the scullery.

The great debate had come to an end. Father Ellis got to his feet, shook his head, patted my mother's arm, winked at Dad, and went into the scullery, with me at his heels.

'Come on, walk with me down the hill,' said the priest to Ronnie. 'There are things you can't get elders to understand.'

Ronnie was standing with his head bent, looking at the boiler. He turned and grabbed up his cap from the back door and went out, preceding the priest, which was very wrong, but under the circumstances could be forgiven him. Once clear of the house we walked abreast, then Father Ellis, putting his arm around Ronnie's shoulder, laughed, 'Don't look so downcast, Ronnie.'

'I'm not downcast, Father.'

'No, you're only annoyed and boiled up inside. Right?'

'Right.'

He didn't add 'Father' and I bit on my lip.

'About this evolution, Ronnie . . .'

Before the priest could go on Ronnie came to a stop and exclaimed, 'I was right, Father.'

'Yes, you were and all.' The priest drew him gently on again, but now his voice sank to a confidential note. 'But man to man, Ronnie, I ask you, do you expect me to explain the theory of evolution to you in front of your mother and dad and the like, and in five minutes? It is a wide subject, deep and wide you must confess, and they have no interest in it whatever at their age.'

He spoke of my mother and dad as if they were very old, but he was the same age as my mother – thirty-two. Dad was three years older but looked much more, that was with being down the pit so long.

We walked in silence for some yards, then Ronnie started again, and he used the tone which he used when he was going to go on talking for a long time. 'About the Garden of Eden, Father. . . .'

'Look . . .' Father Ellis almost pushed him into the ditch, then grabbed his shoulder and pulled him straight again, before throwing back his head and laughing. 'We will have to go into it all another time, right into it, head first into the Garden of Eden, but at the present minute I'm up to my eyes in work. I should never have stayed so long in your house but your mother makes one so comfortable that the time flies and all thought of my duties goes out of my head. But I promise you one of these days we shall get down to evolution and the Garden of Eden. Now I've got to hurry away. But listen, Ronnie, don't you talk about evolution in the kitchen for you'll get them all mixed up – not that I'm suggesting you're mixed up. No, you go on reading about evolution or about anything else you can find in that book of yours, but don't annoy your mother with it.'

He gave Ronnie a gentle punch with his fist then, cupping my chin in his hands, he shook his head saying, 'Here's one who doesn't bother about evolution. Do you, Christine?'

'No, Father.'

'You're too busy living, following the wind in the trees and the voice of the river.'

I wasn't quite sure what he meant, but I replied, 'Yes, Father.'

I expected that Ronnie would be sullen when the priest had gone, but instead he grabbed my hand and, laughing, ran me over the field towards the river, and when we reached the bank and sat down with our feet dangling above the gurgling water, he said to me without looking into my face, 'Do you think I can talk good, Christine?'

'Oh, yes, Ronnie, I love to hear you talk.'

He turned his face quickly to me. 'You do?'

'Yes, I think you're clever, oh, so clever.'

He turned his eyes away and looked across the river and said, 'Some day I will be clever and I'll talk and talk and talk, and I'll make people listen to me. Do you know what I want to do?'

'No.'

He laughed and, turning and kneeling at my side, he grabbed my hand, saying, 'I can always talk to you. I can tell you things. Well, I'll tell you what I want to do. I want to tie people in chairs so that they'll have to listen to me. In the middle of the night I wake up thinking things and nobody wants to listen, so I tie lots of people in chairs, Mam and Dad, Uncle Jim, Mr. Graham' – he was the schoolmaster – 'Aunt Phyllis. Oh, yes, Aunt Phyllis.'

'And me, Ronnie?'

'No, never you, Christine, because you listen. Will you always listen to me, Christine?'

'Yes, always, always.'

That summer the heat was intense and water became scarce, and for only part of the day it ran from the tap in the back-yard. By each evening I would feel so hot and sticky that I would beg my mother once again to let me go in the river with the boys. Ronnie had said he would teach me to swim. But Mam would have none of it.

'You can plodge and that's all,' she said.

So I would plodge in the shallows, shouting across the distance to where the boys sported in the deeper water. They would dive like turtles, the water spraying up like a fountain when they disappeared, then their heads, black and shiny, and their faces running with the cool water would break through a fresh surface. On and on they would go, and I would think, 'Oh, if only. . . .'

At night we didn't go to bed early but sat around with all the doors and windows open. Dad used to sit on the front step reading aloud from the paper while my mother sat at the front window doing her mending or knitting; never did she sit down with idle hands. Gists of his reading stuck in my mind. The Dionne Quins were born, a man who had started to make bicycles with a capital of only five pounds was now a millionaire and they had changed his name from Morris to Nuffield. There was a woman found in a trunk in some station cloakroom, and there had been a lot of jollification over the King's jubilee.

I knew about the jubilee because they had had one or two tea parties in the town, but we hadn't had anything at Fenwick Houses. There had come a tentative suggestion from Mrs. Brown that something should be done for the bairns. 'What,' said my dad, 'and have a means test on the cakes?' Also from his reading I remember there was a man called Hore-Belisha, and he had something to do with lamp-posts, and this made my dad laugh. Then there was another man called Musso who had attacked the poor Abyssinians. Dad said it would be our turn next, and this worried me during a lot of hot, restless nights.

A number of times that summer I walked over Top Fell down to Bertram's Farm with Father Ellis, and Mrs. Bertram always gave me a cup of milk, then asked me, 'Was that nice?' And I always said, 'Yes, thank you.' She had the idea that I was hungry, but I was never hungry. I had only to dash into the house gasping, 'Oh, Mam, I'm starvin',' and my mother would say, 'Well you know where the knife is and you know where the bread is, if you can't help yourself I'm sorry for you.' But I was well aware that this practice wasn't prevalent in Fellburn at that time, and not even in Fenwick Houses, certainly not next door in my Aunt Phyllis's, for both Sam and Don always came in with me when I said I was hungry and always went out with something in their fists.

It wasn't the drink of milk that I looked forward to on these walks with Father Ellis to the farm, but the fun we had.

To my mind he was as good fun as our Ronnie or Sam. I never, even in the vaguest way, coupled Don with Sam, Ronnie and fun, although he was as much my constant companion as the other two.

Once we were on the fells proper, Father Ellis would give me a start, then race me to a tree, or taking my hand he would run and leap me into great leaps, higher than I could jump when I flung my arms round myself. On some of the leaps I could see over the far fells and catch glimpses of the entire town. Sometimes he would tell me a Pat and Mick story, and sometimes I would tell him one, and we both laughed long and loud.

One day, for some reason or another, I had missed him, but I knew he had gone to the farm and I went to meet him. The sun was going down and I stood on the top of High Fell straining my eyes into the dazzling rose and mauve light trying to make him out against the shades on the hills. But I could see nothing, for the sun was making my eyes water. Yet I remember I didn't turn my face away from the light. I was so high up that I felt on top of the sun, and as it slipped over the brow of the hill yon side of the river it seemed so near that I had but to bend forward, put out my hand, and I could press it into the valley beyond.

Blinking, I turned, blinded with colour, to see just a few feet away from me Father Ellis. He was standing looking at me, and I cried joyfully, 'Oh, hallo, Father.' But he didn't speak, he just took my hand and turned away and we walked homewards. I thought he was vexed, somebody had vexed him, yet he didn't look vexed, and then he said in a voice which he only used in confession and never on the fells, 'Christine, how old are you now?'

'Eleven, Father. I was eleven on April the twenty-sixth. You know I was born the day the Duke and Duchess of York were married. It was a nice day to be born, wasn't it?'

I looked up at him and he smiled and said, 'There wasn't a better.' And then he went on, 'But now, Christine, you're a big girl and you must give over dreaming.' He gave a little gentle wag to my hand. 'You must do practical things. You understand what I mean?'

'Yes, Father,' I said, but I wasn't quite sure in my mind.

'You must help your mother with the housework and things in the home, for she works very hard.'

'Oh, I do, Father. I do the brasses every Saturday morning, and the fender – oh, the fender, Father.' I smiled up at him. 'It's awful to do and takes so long to get bright.'

'Yes, I know you do things like that, but you must do even more. You must learn to cook and do all the housework, and sew, and always keep busy.'

'I'm a good sewer, Father, but I don't like patching.'

He laughed now and said, 'No, you wouldn't like patching.' Then he stopped, and looking down at me again with a straight face, he said quietly, 'But you'll remember what I said and try to put your mind on everyday things?'

'Yes, Father.'

I knew what he meant – I was always being told to pay attention and stop dreaming. But I liked dreaming, I liked to lie in bed and float away out of the bed. Not that I didn't like my bed and my little room, and not that I didn't think our kitchen the finest kitchen in the world, but I just wanted to go off somewhere. Where, I couldn't have explained, it was just somewhere. I came near to a vague understanding of this feeling the following spring.

Following the hot summer it was a hard winter, there was a lot of snow, with high winds and great drifts and thaws and freezing, and this pattern seemed to go on for ever. I wasn't very fond of the snow, for my hands, even with gloves on, would become very cold while playing snowballs, and I hated to be rolled in the snow. Our Ronnie knew this and never pushed me into it, nor did Sam, and Sam could have because, although he wasn't tall, he was strong. But Don, at every opportunity, pushed me down and tried to roll me in the snow. This often ended in a fight between Ronnie and him.

One day the fight became grim and Sam joined in, not to help his brother but to help Ronnie, and later that evening I heard Sam getting a walloping and knew Don had told on him. It was during this bitter cold time that I first noticed my mother walking slower. When she came up the hill she would stop once or twice, and as soon as she got in she would sit down. This was unusual, for she never sat down unless it was in the evening. She would never let me carry the bags of groceries, saying they were too heavy for me, nor had she ever let anyone else carry them. But one day she came in and Sam was with her, and he was carrying the big bass bag. It was nearly as big as himself and when he dumped it on the table she looked at him with a smile and said, 'Thanks, Sam.' And Sam's reply was an unusually lengthy one for him, for he said, 'That's all right, Aunt Annie, I'll always carry your bags for you if you like.'

My mother's smile broadened, and she patted his back and said, 'Go in the pantry and cut yourself a shive.'

He turned eagerly away, but then quickly looking back at her said, 'I didn't do it for that, Aunt Annie.'

'No, no, lad, I know that. Go on and don't be so thin-skinned.'

Christmas came but it did not seem so happy this year. The eons of time passed until one morning I knew it was spring. The sun was hard and bright; I had run up to the edge of the wood and there through the trees I saw a wonderful sight. There had been no snow for weeks, but sprinkled around the roots of the trees was something that looked like snow. As far as my eye could see there was this sprinkling of purity white, each drop separate from its fellow and divided within itself, and each part shining. I took in a great gulp of air. I wanted to share this wonder with someone, someone who needed wonder, and who needed wonder at this moment more than my mother, for she was tired. And so, dashing back down the street, I flew into the kitchen where she was on the point of lifting the big black frying pan from the fire, and clinging on to her apron I cried, 'Mam, come up to the wood and see something, it's beautiful. It's been snowing in the wood.'

She turned very quickly and looked down at me with a surprised, almost frightened expression. Then she said sharply, 'Don't be silly, child, it hasn't snowed for weeks.'

Now I laughed at her and said, 'It has, Mam.' I turned my head to where Dad had come out of the scullery, his shirt neck tucked in and soap on his face ready for a shave, and after looking at my face for a moment he said to my mother, 'Go on, lass. Leave the pan, I'll see to it.'

'What!' she exclaimed. 'Don't be silly.'

Now my dad came forward looking as if he had grown old

43

overnight, for the soap had formed a white beard, and taking the pan from her hand he whispered, 'Keep it up.' Then nudging her, he added, 'Go on.'

She looked at me impatiently. 'Oh, come on,' she said, straightening her apron and clicking her tongue.

Her attitude didn't dampen my spirits and I danced before her up the street and into the wood. Then from my vantage point I stopped, and when she came and stood by my side I pointed and she looked. Then her hand came slowly round my shoulder and she pressed me to her.

And as we stood like this, gazing spellbound at the first sprinkling of anemones, I said, 'They seem glad to be out, Mam, don't they?' Her hand drew me closer and she said, 'Yes, hinny, they're glad the winter's over.' Then much to my surprise she didn't turn homeward but walked quietly on into the wood, her arm still around me.

At one point she turned and looked back, and I did, too, wondering what she was looking for. Then she did a strange thing. She went down on her hunkers like my dad did and, taking me by the shoulders, she gazed into my face, her eyes moving around it as if looking for something, like when I've had a flea on me, and pressing my face between her large, rough hands she exclaimed softly, 'Oh, me bairn.' Then she said a thing that was stranger than her kneeling, yet not so strange, for I understood in part. 'Keep this all your life, hinny,' she said. And she ended with something which contradicted a daily statement of hers, for she said, 'Never change. Try to remain as you are, always.'

Now that was a funny thing for her to say for she was forever at me to 'Stop dreaming' and forever saying 'Come on, pay attention'. And hadn't Father Ellis too said that I would have to pay attention. But now she was telling me never to change.

The tears were rolling over the red part of her cheeks and dropping straight on to the grass, and I was crying, too. But it was a quiet crying. Then getting quickly to her feet, she wiped my face round with her apron, then wiped her own and, jerking her head up, she laughed and said, 'Eeh! that frying-pan. Your dad makes a mess of everything. Come on.' And she took my hand. But we didn't run out of the wood, just walked quietly.

44

The spring got warmer and warmer, and everything was beautiful, until I came up the hill one day with Cissie Campbell. She had left school now and had got a job in Braithwaite's the big grocery shop on the High Street that supplied most of Brampton Hill, and she had got very swanky all of a sudden and spoke down her nose. It was just after we had crossed over the bridge and one or two of the men had called, 'Hallo there, Christine,' and I had said, 'Hallo' back and called them by their names that Cissie said, 'I've got something to tell you.' Her voice had dropped to a whisper and she brought her face close to mine. 'You know last Saturday afternoon?' I couldn't remember anything particular about last Saturday afternoon, but I nodded and said, 'Yes.' And she went on, her voice dropping even lower, 'Well, you know what happened? You wouldn't believe it but I was coming across Top Fell, I hadn't reached the top, I was just at that part near the stile where the bushes are, you know that narrow cut?'

Again I nodded.

'Well, I met Father Ellis there and you know what?'

I shook my head now and there was a long pause before she said, 'He tried to kiss me.'

I stopped dead, my eyes stretching upwards, my mouth stretching downwards, even my ears seemed to be stretching out of my head.

'You don't believe me?'

'No, I don't.' I backed from her as if she was the devil himself. 'You're wicked. Priests don't kiss people, not girls. Eeh! Cissie Campbell.'

'He did, I tell you, and I run away.'

'You're lying and I'll tell Mam about you. He's . . . he's holy. My dad says he is the best priest in the world.'

'You promised not to say anything.'

'I didn't.'

'You did.' She was advancing on me now. 'If you dare tell your mother do you know what I'll do?'

I backed again, staring at her all the while.

'I'll tell your mother what you and Don Dowling do down by the river.'

'D . . . D . . . Don.' I was spluttering now, and a little fear was creeping like a thread through my body, vibrating on a

45

memory from the past. 'I've never done anything with Don, never.'

'Yes you have, he told me. And I'll not only tell your mother but I'll go to Father Howard and tell him. And you won't half get it from him if I tell him all Don Dowling told me, so there.'

The many dangers that involved me through Don was security enough for Cissie, but as I watched her stalking away up the hill, her bottom wobbling, I wasn't thinking so much of Don and what he had said about me, but of Father Ellis, and my mind kept repeating, 'He didn't do it, he wouldn't do it.'

The Sunday following this incident my father came into my room very early in the morning and whispered, 'I'm off to mass. Your mother's going to have a lie in this morning, she's not feeling too good. Wouldn't you like to get up and get the breakfast under way?'

I got up and went downstairs and into the front room. Mother was sitting up in bed and she gave me a warm smile as I entered.

'You bad, Mam?'

'No,' she said. 'I took some medicine last night and I've got a pain in my tummy, that's all.'

'Oh.' I let out a long sigh of relief, Epsom Salts always gave me a pain in my tummy.

After getting dressed I set the table for breakfast and then did the vegetables for the dinner, and after Dad came back and breakfast was over I washed up and did the kitchen. With all this I was too late for the ten o'clock mass, the children's mass, so I went to eleven o'clock.

The church was different at eleven o'clock for it was full of grown-ups and all the men seemed to stand at the back while there was still some empty seats at the front. I was sitting behind a pillar and the only way I could see Father Howard was when I craned my neck, and I did crane my neck as he began his sermon, for without any leading up he yelled one word at the congregation.

'Immorality,' he yelled, and then there was such a silence that you could hear people breathing. I did not understand anything of what he said at first until he began to talk about the girls and women of the parish. 'Babylon isn't in it with this town,' he cried, 'and I'm not referring to the prostitutes in Bog's End. They carry out their profession in the open, they don't hide behind religion, nor have they the nerve to come to mass and the sacraments with blackness in their hearts that even they would be ashamed of. This parish has become such that it isn't safe for a priest to walk the streets at night.'

I knew without names being mentioned that the priest Father Howard was referring to was Father Ellis. There was another priest younger than Father Ellis, called Father James, but he did not have a nice face nor a nice voice like Father Ellis. And I also knew that Cissie Campbell had wanted the priest to kiss her and she wasn't the only one, for lots of the grown-up girls were always hanging round him.

When the mass was over and I was going up the side aisle I saw my Aunt Phyllis walking in the throng up the centre aisle; her head was high but her eyes looked downwards, and she had the appearance of someone wrapped around with righteousness. When she saw me outside she seemed surprised and asked, 'Have you been to this mass?' And when I said 'Yes' she said, 'Ah well, I hope it's done you some good.'

Later the whole town was talking about Father Howard's sermon, but neither Dad nor Mam asked me anything about it.

The following year, nineteen-thirty-five, our Ronnie and Don Dowling left school and both started at the Phoenix pit. Dad said it would not make much difference to us as they would dock it off his dole, and they did.

There hadn't been much laughter in our house for some months until one night, sitting at the table, I began to eat slowly, toying with my food, my whole attention concentrated on the thought that had been coming and going in my mind for some long time past. And now, being unable to contain myself any longer as to the truth of Aunt Phyllis's remark, I suddenly raised my eyes and, looking across at Dad, said, 'Have I really got a silly laugh, Dad?'

They all stopped eating and stared at me, then one after the other they began to laugh. My mother first, her body shaking before she would let her laughter loose, Ronnie's mouth was wide and his head back, and Dad, with his two

47

hands clasped on the table, leant across to me – I was now laughing myself – and shaking his head slowly he said, 'It's the best laugh in the land, hinny. Never let it fade ... never.'

That night Ronnie came into my room. I don't know what time it was, I only know that a hand on my shoulder startled me into wakefulness, and I couldn't see anyone in the dark. But then I heard Ronnie's voice whispering near my ear, 'Ssh! it's me.'

I turned on my side in an effort to get up, but his hand kept me still, and I asked, 'What is it? Is Mam bad?'

'No,' he murmured, 'I only wanted to talk to you.'

I screwed my face up in the dark, then said, 'Talk to me? What about?'

'Oh, lots of things,' he whispered. 'I miss you, Christine, now that I'm at work, and we never seem to go anywhere without Sam or Don.' He paused, and although I could only see the dark outline of him I knew that we were staring into each other's eyes. Then, with a little gurgle of merriment in his voice, he asked, 'Have you been worrying about what Aunt Phyllis said that night about your laugh?'

'No,' I lied; 'only I would stop laughing if I thought it was silly.'

'It isn't silly, it's as Dad said, you've got a lovely laugh. And you know somethin', what I heard the day?'

'No.'

'It was when we were on the wagons. Harry Bentop – you wouldn't know him but he's seen you. Well, he said, "By, your sister's not half a smasher, she's going to be the prettiest lass in Fellburn." How d'you like that?'

'Me?'

'Huh, huh.'

I hadn't thought about being pretty. I knew that I had nice hair, everybody said so, but pretty. . . . It was nice to be thought pretty, it was something that I would have to think about, really think about. So went vague thoughts in the back of my mind, but what was bringing me into full wakefulness was a puzzling, bemusing thought, a thought that was there and yet wasn't. It was more of a feeling, and the feeling said that my mother wouldn't like our Ronnie to be here talking to me in the middle of the night.

'I'm sleepy,' I said and, turning abruptly round with a great flounce, I faced the wall.

Some seconds passed before I heard him padding across the room, and although I strained my ears I didn't hear the opening of the door, but knew he was gone by the relieved feeling inside of me.

I could not get to sleep now. Was I going to be the prettiest girl in Fellburn? Did the lads in the pit talk about me? But most of all my mind was groping around the question of why Ronnie had come into my room in the middle of the night to tell me this, why hadn't he told it to me in the kitchen, when Dad and Mam weren't there?

That week-end Ronnie brought home a puppy. He said its name was Stinker, that he would pay the licence and it could live on scraps. This last was to assure mother that it would be no bother as regards food. And lastly he said it was for me. My delight in the gift overflowed from my body and filled the house, and as I took Stinker into my arms, a love sprang up between us that was to make us inseparable until the day he died.

When I was fourteen I asked my mother if I could go to the baths. A number of the girls from school had joined a swimming club, and I had a great urge to learn to swim. I remember she considered thoughtfully for a moment before saying, 'No, Christine, I don't think it wise.'

'But why?' I asked, 'all the girls go, and I'm the only one that can't swim. Ronnie, Don and Sam can swim like ducks and there's me, I have to plodge on the edge. Oh, Mam, let's.'

Again she bowed her head as if considering, then said, 'Not yet awhile, hinny, leave it for a year or so.'

A year or so. In a year or so I'd be old and working, and not wanting to swim. But I didn't upset my mother with my pleading, for she wasn't herself these days, she spent a long time sitting in the lavatory at the bottom of the yard, and when she came into the kitchen she would huddle close to the fire and her face would look grey and drawn. But sometimes for weeks she would be all right, and I would get her to walk in the wood with me, and draw out her laugh with the fantasies I made about the trees. I would point out the oak

and say, 'There it goes making its breadcrumb pudding again.'
This was when it threw its brown, crumbly flowers out in the
spring. Or I'd bring in a spray of horse chestnut, and day
after day give a commentary to her on its unfolding. When
from its scaly brown cloak there peeped a pale reddy-brown
nose, I would turn from the kitchen window where it was
stuck in a jar to cry, 'Look, Mam, it's turned into a ballet
dancer.' And she would come and stand near me and look at
the silver down-engulfed thing straining away from the
brown cloaks that endeavoured to keep it covered. When on
the next day the ballet dancer would be gone, leaving only two
deep olive green leaves, one dangling in folds from a stalk
where the down disappeared at the touch of a finger, so fine
it was, I would continue my story. But she wouldn't, I noticed,
look so much at the wonder of the opening chestnut bud as at
me. In the middle of my narrating, if I turned and looked
up at her it would be to find her eyes riveted on my head,
and the soft, warm, comforting light in them would bring
my attention wholly to her, and I would fling my arms around
her waist and lay my head on her shoulder – now I could do
that, for I was tall for my age. On such days as these I was
wrapped around in a warm comforting glow.

When some months later I again put the plea of learning to
swim to her, she shut me up quickly with a snapping reply, and
I went out and down to the lavatory and had a good cry.
When I returned to the scullery I knew that my father had
come in, and that she had been telling him, for I heard his
voice saying quietly, 'Don't be afraid for her, God has a way
of looking after his own,' and I stood in some bewilderment.
What was she afraid of? Why should she be afraid for me just
because I wanted to learn to swim? Other girls learned to
swim and their mothers weren't afraid for them, at least, I
didn't think so. It should be the other way round; she should
be afraid because I couldn't swim and would likely drown in
the river if I fell in. Her attitude to this matter was very
puzzling. Then one Saturday morning, when I was wrapped
around with the warm glow again and the smell of baking in
the kitchen, she began to talk to me. Not looking at me, she
told me that I mustn't go off on my own with any boys.

'But I don't go around with boys, Mam, you know I don't.'
I was slightly huffed. 'Only with Don and Ronnie and Sam.'

There was a long pause, before she said, 'Well, never go out with Don on your own, always see that Ronnie goes along.'

I didn't want to go off with Don on my own, anywhere, or at any time, but did this rule apply to Sam? So I said, 'Not with Sam, either, Mam?'

'Oh.' She straightened her back. 'Oh, Sam is just a boy.' And she turned and looked at me and smiled warmly at me as she added, 'Sam's all right.'

Well, what was there to worry about? I didn't want to be alone with anybody, only perhaps Stinker when we went over the fells or into the wood. There were times when I was happier with Stinker than with anyone else I could think of. With Stinker as my sole companion I felt free; the closed-in feeling that I had in the company of Ronnie and Don fled and I felt lighter, able to run or sit if I wanted to without the restricting touches of their hands or contact with their bodies.

I had a sense of guilt when I felt that our Ronnie's presence, too, was irksome to me, for I had a nice feeling for him, at least during the day. But not at night when he came creeping into my room and woke me up because he wanted to talk. This had happened twice since that first night, when he told me I was pretty.

Then one day I went to the wood to take, so I told myself, my last walk, for on the morrow I was starting work. This business of starting work held no joy for me, for I was going into Mrs. Turnbull's draper shop. Father Ellis had got me the job. I was to start at quarter to nine in the morning, and four evenings a week I would finish at seven o'clock, but on Saturday it could be eight or nine, all according to custom, Mrs. Turnbull had pointed out. Wednesday I finished at one o'clock. Mother comforted me by saying it might lead to better things. What, I couldn't see, as there was only another girl and Mrs. Turnbull in the business. And the other girl was new, too.

Aunt Phyllis said I was lucky to get a job at all when there were dozens of girls with 'something up top' who would have jumped at the chance, but there was nothing like finding favour in the priest's eyes. And now, she had added, and this was in the absence of my mother, I might stop acting like a wild thing and grow up and have some sense. I knew

51

she was referring to Don and Sam following me about, and I wanted to say to her that I didn't want anybody to follow me about, I would rather be on my own, but I had strict orders from mother never to be cheeky, not to anyone, but particularly not to Aunt Phyllis. When speaking about Aunt Phyllis my mother always finished with, 'She has enough on her plate.'

And so I walked in the wood with Stinker at my heels. He seemed to feel the coming breach, too, for he didn't scamper about among the undergrowth but walked with his tail between his legs and his head cast down. He was taking his cue from my feelings. I went through one bay after the other, and it was when turning to make my way home again from the tree bay that I saw Fitty Gunthorpe.

When I had come across him in the wood following the incident of the rabbit I had run to get out of his way, but now I didn't run, for as on the morning that I had been riveted to the ground at the sight of the nailed rabbit, so I was equally riveted now, for Fitty was looking at something in his hand. It was a small bird. It was bare and had been plucked clean. If it had been large I would have known he had killed a pigeon and was going to eat it, but this was a small bird, too small to eat. Its body looked the size of a tiny mouse. It lay on its back in his great palm, its two spidery little legs sticking up into the air.

As if coming out of a trance Fitty took his eyes from the bird and looked at me, then he dropped it on to the ground, so quickly that it seemed as if someone had shot it from his hand, and he flicked his hand twice as if to throw off contact with the poor thing. Then coming towards me with slow steps, his eyes darting from my face to Stinker, who was growling now, he began to jabber. 'I didn't ... Listen ... listen, I found it. It wasn't me, I've done nothin' to it. ... You're the one that s ... s ... said about the r ... rabbit ... aren't you?'

I could only stare unblinking into his face. He was standing an arm's length from me now, and I was terrified. Then he frightened me still further by flinging his arms wide and crying, 'You've ... you've got to listen, see. I found it. I tell you I found it, it was still warm. Somebody's plucked it, not me, not me. I swear by Christ, not me!' Then his manner changed, and his voice dropped to a whining whisper, as he pleaded, 'Don't say anythin', will you? They'll say it was me. It wasn't me. Please, for Christ's sake, don't say anythin'.'

I backed from him, and when he cried again, his voice breaking as if on the verge of tears, 'Don't, will you?' I shook my head in a sickly daze and whispered, 'No, no, I won't.' Then I turned and went out of the wood, not running, yet not walking. But when I reached the top of the street, away from the shadow of the trees, I had my work cut out not to fly into our house and cry, 'The poor bird! the poor bird!'

I said nothing about the bird to anyone, not because I was thinking of Fitty, but because I was seeing his father's face as he had looked at me all those years ago. . . .

Next morning I presented myself at a quarter to nine at Mrs. Turnbull's shop. Dad had gone with me to the bridge, and before leaving me he had grinned down at me, saying, 'Well, lass, you are on your own now, life starts from this mornin'. Away you go now.' With a pressure of his hand he pushed my reluctant body across the bridge, and now here I was, confronted by Mrs. Turnbull and meeting, for the first time, Mollie Pollock.

Mrs. Turnbull was a short woman, and very fat. She seemed to me to be all large bumps, and strangely enough Mollie Pollock too was short and fat, but her fat didn't appear like bumps, it was more like molten flesh, pouring continuously from some central point of her body, for ever mobile.

Mrs. Turnbull informed us both abruptly and without any preamble that we had a lot to learn and we had better get started. The shop had two compartments but only one entrance. Into the second compartment she led me, and placed on the counter, apparently all ready for me, were numerous boxes, some holding cards of buttons, and others, a jumble of coloured tapes and bobbins of thread. My first duty was to get these all sorted out and counted, and to label anew the boxes, which had their place in a high framework that formed the dividing wall of the shop.

There was no window in the second compartment, only a skylight, and I found my eyes drawn to this time and again. The first hour seemed like an eternity, and I had my work cut out not to take to my heels and fly out of the place, for I felt I couldn't breathe. The air was thick, the smell was thick, it was what I called a calico smell.

At eleven o'clock Mrs. Turnbull brought me a mug of cocoa. This, too, was thick and I couldn't drink it. All morning I sorted buttons, tapes and threads and wrote labels, and the latter didn't suit Mrs. Turnbull, my writing was too large and sprawly, and a number of the labels I had to do again. Also I had spelt button 'buttin'. She was very sharp with me about this.

My dinner hour break was from quarter past twelve until one o'clock; it took almost twenty minutes hard walking from the shop to our house, which left only a few minutes for a meal. My mother asked me somewhat anxiously how I got on, and I could not dispel the hope in her eyes by telling her the truth, that I hated the shop, so I just answered weakly, 'All right.' Dad patted my head and said, 'There, lass, it's a new world.'

Yes, indeed it was a new world.

By the end of the week it was decided that I must stay in the town for my dinner, so Mam put me up a packet of sandwiches. I told her I could sit in the back shop and eat them, and this I did for the first two days of the new arrangement, until Mollie whispered to me in passing one morning, 'I'm bringin' me dinner an' all, but I'm going to have it in the park. You comin'?' Instinctively, I nodded, 'Yes.' And a feeling of excitement arose in me at the prospect of being able to sit in the park without being accompanied by any one of the boys.

From that dinner-time Mrs. Turnbull's shop took on a lighter shade. And the credit for this was due solely to Mollie, for she, even at sixteen, was a character. But she was a character my mother would certainly not have liked me to associate with, had she known how Mollie spoke.

There was very little swearing went on in our house. Outside, men swearing was as natural as a 'God bless you'. But women who swore were not nice, and I had been warned not to stand and listen to women who talked like this, as the lads would do.

But here was Mollie, swearing and cursing with nearly every other word she spoke, and it did not stop me from liking her. The strange thing about it was I found myself wanting to laugh as I listened to her, although I must admit her opening comment on our employer not only startled me but almost choked me, for I was swallowing a mouthful of meat and bread at the moment Mollie exclaimed in a doleful tone, 'Doesn't fat-arse Turnbull give you the pip?'

When she had thumped my back until I had spat out the meat, I sat up on the bench and we looked at each other, then we burst into gales of laughter. From that moment we were friends.

She informed me that this was the fifth job she'd had in a year, and if she lost this her mother would bash her brains in. Moreover, that she had only got it because her sister lived in Norton Terrace and was respectable, her husband being a bus driver. Mollie herself lived in Bog's End and was one of eleven children. Her father, when in work, was a ragman. But now, as she said, everybody was in bloody rags, so business was at a standstill.

It was strange that I could sit listening to Mollie swearing and cursing and not once think, Eeh! she's awful, or Eeh! she's bad. Mollie was a natural swearer – there are such people who space the words into their own language and so colour it. It is, in a way, a gift, and she was the only one I ever met who had it, for when Cissie Campbell said even 'Damn and blast!' something would curl up inside of me against the repulsive sound, but not so with Mollie, Yet, nevertheless, I did not take Mollie home, for I knew immediately what my mother would say. She would find no entertainment or charm in Mollie's language, and I had no doubt about what would have been her attitude had she known that I was listening to it every day.

Sitting on the park seat in the bright sunlight one dinner hour, Mollie turned to me and said, 'Eeh! Christine, you know, you are bonny.' I felt my cheeks broadening with pleasure, but I denied the statement, saying, 'I'm not really, it's only me hair,' and I tossed over my shoulder one of my two plaits. 'It isn't only your hair,' went on Mollie, 'your hair's got nowt to do with it really, it's your face. The shape of it, and your eyes.' Then she leaned back against the park seat and, hanging her hands over the rail, she surveyed me and exclaimed, 'My God! what I wouldn't give to have your eyes. I'd run bare skinned round the bloody shipyard for them. Y'know what?' She had come up close to me now, lowering her voice, 'You could marry a bloody duke!'

When my laugh rang out, she shook my arm, saying, 'I'm not jokin', Christine,' although she was herself laughing, 'honest to God, you could! Coo, if I had your face, Fellburn wouldn't see me backside for dust.'

Now I was laughing louder and louder, and, warming to her theme, Mollie ranted on telling me what she would do if she was me.

That night I lit a new candle and stared at my face in the small mirror on top of the chest of drawers, the only article of furniture, beside the single bed, which the room would hold. My face looked waxy and pale and somehow far away. I moved nearer to the glass and stared into my eyes, but they didn't seem to stare right back at me, they looked dreamy, and I gurgled to myself, 'They're not paying attention.' And my eyes weren't paying attention to me, they were looking deep inside me, right into the place where my dreams were. For now, strangely enough since I had started work, I was dreaming more and more. In the mornings, surrounded by tapes, bobbins and bales of flannelette and drill, I released myself from the shop and went straight up through the fanlight into my dream world, the dream world which held the river and the wood and fells, and ... someone. This someone who was big, yet had no definite outline. He was no one that I knew, not even Father Ellis, but he was someone beautiful to look upon, someone who spoke with a soft voice, a caressing voice, someone who kept saying, 'Christine, oh, Christine.' And this someone had no resemblance to our Ronnie, oh no, none whatever, although Ronnie kept saying, 'Christine, oh, Christine.'

There had lately come into me a fear when I heard our Ronnie speaking my name like that, and he was doing it more and more, for he was always wanting to talk to me in the night. He had never touched me or sat on my bed. He just squatted on his hunkers by the side of the bed and talked and talked in whispers. Yet fear of his visits was growing in me and I was terrified lest my mother should find out, for somehow I knew she would blame me. Yet I kept asking myself, why, why should she?

I had been at Mrs. Turnbull's a year when I got a shilling a week rise, which brought my wages to eight and sixpence, and because of this I was detailed to do a job for which I had no taste. This was going round the other shops in the centre of the town and taking note of their prices. If they were selling winceyette at one and threepence three-farthings a yard, Mrs. Turnbull would alter her card to one and three-pence-farthing. She was the first of the cut-price shops, I think.

It was on one of these distasteful excursions that I ran into Don. He wasn't in his working clothes, but had on his good suit and looked very big and hefty and, I noticed for the first time, somewhat handsome.

'Where you off to?' he asked, surprised to see me out.

When I told him he laughed and said, 'Well, she's got her head screwed on all right, I must say that for her. Look, come on and have a cup of tea.'

'No, no, I can't, Don,' I protested; 'I've got to get back, she'll raise the roof if I'm late.'

'Let her.' He was looking at me from the depths of his dark eyes. I could almost feel the gaze coming out of them, sharp and piercing, going through my clothes, right through my skin.

When I turned away, saying again, 'No, Don, I can't,' he pulled me back without moving a step. He just reached out with his great arm, and there I was, standing where I had been a second before, looking at him. Then without any leading up, as was the custom with lads, even this much I knew without having had experience, he said, 'This is as good a place as any to tell you, you're goin' to be me girl.'

I strained back from him, unable for a moment to say anything to this straight statement. Then vehemently I declared, 'Oh, no, I'm not, Don Dowling!'

At this he laughed and sang softly, 'Won't you come home, Bill Bailey?' then added, 'That's how you said that. Oh, no, you're not, Don Dowling! Well, I am, and you are, Christine Winter, do you hear?'

There were people passing us in the street now and looking at us, and he turned me about as if I was a cloth doll and led me down a cut that gave on to the town boat landing. I wriggled in his grip and cried, 'Don't be silly, Don, leave go!' But he took no notice until we were standing on the empty landing, the river flowing coldly by, and then he said, without any laughter now, 'I'm sick of this. What does

57

your mam expect? Does she think you're going to end up in a convent? And there's your Ronnie an' all gettin' as bad as her.'

'I don't want any lad. And Mam says I'm too young, I'm only fifteen. . . . Anyway,' I added with some spirit, 'you'll not be my lad, Don Dowling.'

'Now look here, Christine,' his voice was softer now, 'don't take that line. I know it's not you talkin', you want to come out with me all right, but it's your mother, isn't it? God damn! you've got to come alive sometime, she's got to let you come alive.' Now his voice fell to a low, angry tone as he finished, 'She can't keep you in blinkers all the time.'

'Leave me go, leave me go!' I pulled away from him. 'My mother doesn't keep me in blinkers. And I don't want a lad, you or anybody else, so there!'

I turned from him and again he was blocking my way, and now his voice and manner changed once more and he was pleading, his words running into one another. 'Look, Christine, don't be mad. I'll do anything for you, anything, and I won't always be down the pit. No, by God! I've got something else in view. I'll have money some day, Christine, and I'll dress you up.' He spread his hands, making an outline about me but without touching me. 'Only be nice to me, Christine, let me see you alone sometimes.'

I had never before heard him plead, and it didn't seem like him, and I could have felt sorry for him, but I said, and quite firmly, 'I don't want you for a lad, Don. Why, you're more like me brother.'

'All right,' he said, his voice definite, 'I'll be your brother. Only don't keep avoiding me. I'll play the brother – anything you want.'

'But, Don, don't be silly, you can't.' I was trying to get past him as I spoke, and suddenly he brought me close to him, and with his face almost touching mine he muttered, 'But Ronnie does, doesn't he? He plays the brother all right. Oh,' he gave me a shake, 'don't tell me what I know. And when we are on, there's little Sam – dear little Sam. You don't mind sneaking off into the wood with Sam, do you? And don't tell me he's still at school and only a kid. Aye, he's only a kid but he's all eyes and quivers where you're concerned.' He shook me again, and then exclaimed, 'You've played fast and loose with the lot of us for years and it's finished.'

'Let me go, do you hear, let me go! If you don't I'll tell Aunt Phyllis.'

This threat brought his head up and he emitted a hard laugh. 'You'll tell Aunt Phyllis, and do you know what she'll say? She'll say you're a liar, she's always said you were a liar, and she'll go to your mother and she'll tell her to stop you from running after me and trying to trap me. Go on, tell Aunt Phyllis.'

'Here, what's up, what's he doing to you, lass?' The man's voice seemed to come out of the water, and when I turned my startled gaze towards his head which showed just above the landing stage the appeal in my eyes brought him up quickly and across the landing, crying, 'Leave her be!'

When Don's hold relaxed on my shoulder and he turned round to confront the man, my legs seemed too weak to hold me and I staggered a moment before turning to run. The last I heard as I dashed up the alleyway was the man shouting, 'You try it on an' you'll find yersel' in the river.'

I wanted to tell my mother of the incident but I was scared, for she would surely go into Aunt Phyllis and then there would be a row and Sam wouldn't be allowed to come in. Strangely enough it was this last that stopped me from confiding in her. Sam's only refuge was our house, for never a day went by but Aunt Phyllis's hand and voice were raised against him, and more so of late because she knew that when he came out of school he met my Uncle Jim. Uncle Jim was now living openly with the woman in the sweet shop, and it was to Sam that he gave the money for Aunt Phyllis, and always when Sam put the money on the table Aunt Phyllis pelted him with questions, then usually accused him of telling lies like his father, and the result of this would be Sam getting his ears boxed.

I doubt, too, if I had told my mother everything, whether she would have believed me utterly, for that night Don came into our kitchen and he acted as if nothing at all had happened, in fact, as if we were on the best of terms. First of all he joked banteringly with Ronnie, saying, 'You'll never believe it, Ronnie, but old Threadgold is putting me up for deputy. He says I've got all it takes.' Then, turning to my mother, he said, 'In five years' time I'll be a manager, how about that for success, Aunt Annie? And all due to the boy's brains.'

Ronnie laughed, as did my father, but my mother only smiled and said, 'Well I suppose there's stranger things happen.' Then just before he took his leave he said to Ronnie, 'Did you hear Father Ellis's running a social a week come Saturday?'

'No,' said Ronnie. 'Who told you?'

'Jonesy asked me did I want any tickets, and I bought a couple.' Then turning from Ronnie, he looked straight at my mother and with a disarming smile he said, 'Will it be all right for Christine to come along, Aunt Annie?'

My mother blinked twice, then lowered her gaze quickly to the mat before turning to me. The look on my face must have puzzled her for she replied neither 'Yes' nor 'No', but left the decision to me, saying, 'Well, it's up to Christine. If she wants to go to the social, she can.'

'We'll all go.' Ronnie had stood up.

'That's settled then,' said Don. He gave a nod that included us all. 'So long.'

'So long.'

As soon as the door had closed on him I turned to my mother, saying hurriedly under my breath, 'I'm not going to the social.'

'Why not? I thought—' She looked at me closely.

'I just don't want to go.'

'All right, all right, me girl, if you don't want to go you needn't.'

I knew she was puzzled, for I had been on to her for some weeks to let me go to the dances that were run in the schoolroom on a Saturday night, and of which I had heard from time to time such glowing and romantic accounts. A social, of course, was different. At a social, because of the old people and the very young, you played whist and games and just had a dance or two. Don had been clever in picking on a social. Don was clever altogether. His cleverness at this moment filled me with fear – who would have thought that only this morning he had acted like someone mad on the boat landing?

That night Ronnie came into my room again. It wasn't so very late and I wasn't asleep, and he sat on his hunkers by the bed and whispered, 'What's up, Christine?'

'Nothing,' I said. 'What makes you think that?'

'There's something wrong. I saw your face when Don was on about the social. Has he been at you?'

I could see the outline of him bending forward, and when his hand came on to my shoulder I shrugged it off, moving over to the wall, and I turned the conversation by saying, 'Look, our Ronnie, if me mam knew you were coming in here she would get mad.'

'Why should she, I'm doin' nothing? Good lord' – his whisper was intense – 'can't I just talk to you?'

His words sounded so reasonable that I felt silly. Silence fell between us, heavy and thick as the gloom in the room, and then he whispered, 'Don't think I'm sayin' anything against Don, but keep clear of him, Christine. Promise me. Do you hear me?'

'How can I promise when I don't know what you mean,' I stalled, knowing full well what he meant, and also knowing there was no need to extract a promise from me.

'Don't go out with him alone, he's wantin' to take up with you. Do you like him?'

'No, and you know I don't.'

I heard him sigh. Then after a pause he said, 'But that could only make him keener. He likes them hard to get, makes him feel tough. And he is tough, he might make you go out with him.'

I hitched myself up in the bed and my whisper carried all the conviction in me, 'I'll never go out with Don Dowling, never. And you can tell him that if you like.' After a moment I felt him rising, and then he whispered, 'Good night.'

I wondered if my mother would be surprised if I asked for a bolt on my door, and my last thoughts before I went to sleep were, 'Don't be silly, you can't ask for a bolt on the door. . . .'

In spite of all my protests that I didn't want to go to the social, I went after all. Two things contributed to my final decision. One was the pressure of Ronnie, and the other, which more than weighted the balance of the scales, a dress which my mother brought back from Mrs. Durrant's. It was an evening dress of pale blue velvet, and when my mother held it up before her I exclaimed in admiration, 'Oh! don't cut it up, Mam, wear it.'

'What!' my mother exclaimed, 'with no back to it?' She

glanced merrily at Dad. 'That would be the day, wouldn't it?' He nodded but declared gallantly, 'There wouldn't be a bonnier back shown at the do.'

There was a lot of laughter, followed by a lot of talk about just how she was going to alter the dress. The result of her handiwork was something quite beyond my dreams. She made the neck what she called 'low'. This meant that the line came below the nape and allowed my gold crucifix that had belonged to my great-grandmother to lie just below the hollow. The sleeves did not reach my elbow and were trimmed with minute flowers she had unpicked from the original belt. The skirt was full and reached below my calves, and the bodice she made in a wrap-over style. Why she chose this shape I didn't question. There was at the time nothing to question. It was Don who said, some years later, 'She even padded your front so we wouldn't know you had breasts.'

I had asked Mrs. Turnbull if I might be let off early on the Saturday night, and this privilege she grudgingly granted. Mollie, too, wanted to come to the social, but she would not let Mollie off.

At six o'clock I dashed out of the shop and through Fell-burn and up the hill, and I was panting and red in the face when I reached the kitchen. My mother had all my things ready and she followed me up to my bedroom. There was as much excitement as if it was for my wedding.

When later I stood in the kitchen turning myself round before Dad's gaze I had a mighty surge of pleasurable happiness. I was for the first time acutely aware of myself as a whole, I had a body that did justice to my face and hair, and the feeling felt good.

There was a softness in Dad's eyes that was almost moisture as he gazed at me without speaking. Then he said softly, 'Lass, you're a picture come to life.'

'Oh, Dad.' I shook my head at him, but nevertheless felt greatly pleased, not so much with the words he had spoken as with the depth of feeling with which he uttered them.

Ronnie, standing by the table, had said nothing, and this was taken for brotherly indifference. He was wearing a blue serge suit which my mother had got him last year through the store club, and now the sleeves were a little too short, although my mother had turned down the cuffs as she had also done the turn-ups of the trousers. Yet he looked nice; he looked like my dad must have looked at his age, but already he was much taller than Dad.

My mother was once again adjusting my dress and patting the folds into place when there came a tap on the outer door, and she shouted 'Come in'.

Don came in, followed by Sam. Don had on a blue serge suit and it looked new. He was wearing, I noticed, new shoes, too, and over his arm he carried his mack, also new. Everything about him looked so startlingly new that an exclamation was forced from my mother, and she said, 'Why, Don, aren't we smart the night! Has your ship come in?'

He moved the mack from one arm to the other, straightened his tie and said, 'Not a ship yet, Aunt Annie, just a little sculler.'

I saw Dad look at him. Our Ronnie and Don received the same wage; we were in a better position altogether than Aunt Phyllis, yet our Ronnie could not have a new suit.

As Don answered my mother he did not look at her but at me. Although I was standing sideways to him I knew that his eyes were moving all over me, yet he never said a word. It was Sam who, coming and standing in front of me, looked up into my face with a look that was to grow and deepen with the years, and hurt me with its tenderness and frighten me in a particular way with its adoration. Now his eyes tight on mine, not on the dress, he said in awe-laden tones, 'Eeh! Christine, you look lovely.'

I did not deny this as I had done to Dad, or would have done if Don or Ronnie had said it, but I answered him softly, 'Do I, Sam?'

'Aye,' he nodded, and then he looked to where Dad was standing near the fire, and my father and he smiled at each other knowingly.

'Well if we're going we'd better be moving unless we want to meet them coming out.' It was our Ronnie speaking and somewhat impatiently. I walked into the front room, my mother following, and there she helped me on with my coat; then turning me round towards her and flicking an imaginary speck from my shoulder and adjusting the cross on my neck, she said softly, 'Enjoy yourself, lass.' Yet her tone did not convey the meaning of the words, rather it held a warning, but she continued to smile. Then accompanied by Dad, too, now, I followed Ronnie and Don.

Self-consciously I stepped out into the street and there, at her door, stood Aunt Phyllis. I smiled at her but she did not return my smile. She could see most of my dress through my open coat, yet she didn't make any comment on it, but looking towards Don, she snapped, 'Mind, I'm not waitin' up all night for you.' Then seeing Sam standing behind me and in front of Mam and Dad on the step, she said, 'Come on in here, I've been looking for you.'

I walked away down the street between Don and Ronnie. At the corner, leaning against the wall with two or three other men, was Mr. Patterson from next door. He was chewing a long piece of straw, and he pulled it quickly from his mouth and exclaimed, 'By! Christine, you're a smasher the night. Off to enjoy yersel'?'

'Yes, Mr. Patterson, I'm going to the social.'

'That's it, lass, enjoy yersel' when you're young. You're old afore you know it. Life flees. We're nowt but Feathers in the Fire.'

As we walked on Don muttered under his breath, 'Feathers in the fire. Old afore you know it. He makes me sick. That lot were never young. It won't happen to me.'

Ronnie, leaning across me, inquired jokingly of him, 'What are you going to do, take monkey glands?'

'Aye, monkey glands it'll be, but in the form of money. Money is all the monkey glands a feller needs. Money will keep me young, I'll see to that.'

Ronnie's eyes were narrow now, and he looked Don up and down before saying, 'Well, it looks as if you've had your first dose. Where did you get the windfall to buy that lot?'

Now Don's head went back and he moved it in stiff, slow movements from side to side. 'That's my business. I gave you the chance last week to be in on a good thing, but no, didn't want to dirty your fingers.'

Ronnie's face was stiff now and his voice resembled a growl as he said, 'I'm not gettin' meself into trouble doing any shady business.'

'It's not shady; it's business, but it's not shady. If you buy somethin' for threepence and sell it for sixpence that's business, there's nowt shady about it.'

'All right, have it your own way but—'

'Look. Are you going to this social or a boxing match, just let me know?' The words sounded cool; my tone was a grown-up tone. I felt grown-up, the dress was having an effect. Anyway, my attitude checked them both for they hesitated in their walk and laughed. Then, as if both of the same mind, they suddenly grabbed my hands and ran me down the hill as if we were children again, and in this moment of anticipation and excitement I did not resent the feeling of Don's hand in mine.

Just before we came in sight of the bridge they jerked to a stop and as I billowed out from them like a balloon about to take off I wrenched my hands free. Then I, too, came to a halt on the sight of two lads – no, lads is not the right word, young men can only describe them. It was these two young men who had halted Don and Ronnie. They were surveying us from a rise just off the road. They were both dressed in grey flannels and sports coats and wound around their necks were long scarves.

To wear woollen scarves in the height of summer seemed ridiculous, yet they did not look ridiculous; in fact I thought it was we three who must be appearing ridiculous for they both were looking at us through narrowed lids in a scrutinizing, weighing-up fashion, as if we were some oddities that they could not really make out. But I felt no feeling of resentment that they should look at us in this manner, rather my feeling was one of interest, for in a peculiar way the taller of the two seemed to be known to me. His face was pale; what colour his eyes were I could not see from this distance, I only knew they were bright and dark. His hair was brown and had a slight wave in it, and his body was thin, very thin, and he was as tall as Don.

When we had passed them Don spoke. 'They make me sick,' he said, sneering.

I turned my eyes swiftly to our Ronnie as he endorsed this in much the same tone.

'Who are they?' I asked.

'Cissies,' replied Don, 'from Brampton Hill. They're still at school and they wear them scarves to let you know it. I would like to swing them by their scarves, I would that.'

'You mean college?' I said, with a spark of interest.

'Call it what you like it's still school, and these are the types that get the jobs with the money. My God!' he spat into the gutter, and I closed my eyes for a moment and gave a little shiver.

Ronnie, sensing my feelings, put it cheerfully now, 'Ah well, let's live for the night. Away to the social and the high life of Fellburn.' He laughed and was about to link my arm when he thought better of it, thinking that whatever he did Don would do the same.

Ten minutes later I was standing at the school-room door being greeted by Father Ellis.

'Christine! Well, well.' His eyes looked me over. 'A new dress. Did ... did your mother make it?'

'Yes, Father.' I was feeling now slightly embarrassed, for he had not lowered his voice and it had attracted the attention of most of the lads standing just within the doorway. They were buttoning and unbuttoning their coats. Among the eyes that were looking at me were those of Ted Farrel. Ted had been 'a big boy' at school when I had just left the infants, and I had always liked the look of him, and seeing him now close by and not with the width of the church between us, where I glimpsed him on a Sunday, I found that my opinion hadn't changed.

I turned my face away from the eyes and looked at the school clock. It said twenty-five past seven. The social would go on until half past ten. Three hours of enchantment lay before me. . . .

At half past nine I was back home standing in the kitchen looking with desperate eyes at my mother. Ronnie was standing with downcast head. The sleeve of his jacket was hanging off and he was bleeding from the nose and a cut on the chin.

'What ... what in the name of God's happened?' asked Dad.

Mam had said nothing, and I burst out crying and ran upstairs. In a few minutes she was with me and she pulled me up from the bed where I had flung myself and helped me off with my dress. She never spoke until she had folded the dress and put it away in the bottom drawer. Then drawing me down on to the side of the bed she took my hand in hers and said quietly, 'Tell me about it, lass.'

With my eyes cast down and my head moving from side to

side I muttered, 'It was Don, he didn't want me to dance with anybody else. A boy called Ted – Ted Farrel asked me and Don said if – if I danced with him again he would . . .'

'Go on,' said my mother.

'He – he would make him so's his mother wouldn't know him.'

'What did Ronnie do?' asked my mother. 'Did he know of this?'

'He – he . . .' I found I couldn't say that Ronnie, too, had warned me not to dance with Ted Farrel. How could I explain to her the grip on my arm as we went stumbling round the room, and him whispering, 'Now look, I'm tellin' you, our Christine. Don't you encourage Ted Farrel, for he's got a name. He's no good, and there'll only be trouble.'

'Where did they fight?'

'I – I don't know, I think it was near the boiler house. I saw Ted go out with two pals and then Don said to our Ronnie, "Come on".'

'Where was Father Ellis in all this?'

'In the whist. Somebody told him and he came out and stopped them, and . . . Oh, Mam!' I fell on her neck, 'everybody was looking at me, as if – as if . . .'

'There, there. Look – look at me.'

When I raised my eyes she said, 'Do you like Don, even a little bit?'

'No, Mam. No . . . no!'

She drew in a deep breath, then exclaimed, 'Thank God for that. I knew you didn't as a bairn, but girls change you know, and often in their teens they . . . well, they . . .'

'I could never like Don, I – I'm afraid of him, Mam.'

Her eyes tightened on mine and she said sternly, 'Don't be afraid of him, that's what he wants. Don is not a good boy, Christine. There's something, I don't know what it is, but there's something I can't fathom about him.'

I knew what she meant, and when she said next, 'You must keep out of his way as much as possible,' I didn't reply but asked myself somewhat wildly how I could do that, living almost in the same house with him?

Sensing my feelings, my mother said, 'I know, lass, it's going to be difficult.' Then she added, 'And we don't want any open rift if we can help it. Aunt Phyllis is a funny customer,

67

I know, and she would try the patience of a saint, but she's got a lot on her plate. She's a very unhappy woman, so we don't want to make things worse for her. Just you keep him at arm's length, and whatever you do don't let him see you're afraid of him.'

We looked at each other in the flickering candle-light, then her hands came out and cupped my face, and as she stared at me her eyes grew very soft, and bending forward she kissed me on the mouth. This was a very unusual gesture. I kissed her every night before going to bed and also before going out in the morning, but it was on the side of her cheek, and when she kissed me it was on my cheek, but this was a special kind of kiss and in that moment I felt that I must always be good and never, never do anything that would hurt her.

CHAPTER THREE

I REMEMBER the day I left Mrs. Turnbull's. It was a day in October, nineteen-thirty-eight, shortly after Hitler over-ran Czechoslovakia. I knew about this from Dad's talk, for I did not read the papers. He had been very concerned about this man called Hitler, but now, seemingly, the man had got what he wanted and everything would settle down. Anyway they had stopped digging trenches in the London parks.

Mollie, on the other hand, took a great interest in the news-papers and gave me her verdict, day by day, on the headlines. I knew that she was disappointed there wasn't going to be a war. A war for Mollie meant excitement and all the lads in uniform.

She was talking, this particular morning, in whispers and with some regret about the latest news, saying, 'Eeh! by, me ma had some fun in the last war. She keeps me in stitches sometimes with the things she did. And she had some chances an' all. She was a bloomin' fool not to snap one of 'ems up, sergeants and the like. And then she had to go and marry me da. That was a case of must. By, I've learned somethin'. If there was another war no bloody tatie peelin' private would get me, I can tell you. I mayn't be a Greta Garbo but I've got me head screwed on the right way. By, I have. Me ma's taught me a lesson, and the squad she's got.'

'Wouldn't you marry a pitman?'

'Pitman? Not me. No bloody fear. Pitman!'

I looked at her out of the side of my eye and said with a little laugh, 'I thought you liked our Ronnie?'

She gave me a sly look back, dug me in the ribs and said, 'Likin's one thing, marryin's another. If he won the pools now, I'd have him the morrer.'

We both burst out laughing, then covered our laughter

hurriedly as we heard Mrs. Turnbull coming out of the other shop. I remember I turned from a shelf to look at her and my mouth fell into a gape, for behind her stood Dad. He came straight towards me, his cap moving nervously between his hands, and said, 'I've been talking to Mrs. Turnbull' – he nodded his head back at her – 'you'll have to come home, lass, your mother's taken bad.'

I said nothing, I did not even apologize to Mrs. Turnbull for my hasty exit, but, running out to the back, I grabbed up my coat and hat and joined Dad in the shop. And there, Mollie, before Mrs. Turnbull could speak, asked, 'Will you be comin' back?'

It was my dad who answered. 'I don't think so, lass, not yet. Me wife's very ill, she'll be in bed for some time.'

Mrs. Turnbull moved with us towards the door, where she said, 'I'm very sorry, very sorry indeed, Mr. Winter.' And turning to me she finished, 'Your situation's waiting for you when you can come back, I'll see to that.'

'Thank you,' I said, and hurried into the street. And there gabbled my questions at Dad: What was the matter? When did it happen? How did it happen? What was it? She was all right when I left this morning.

Apparently my Aunt Phyllis had sent someone to the allotment for him, and when he got back he found my mother in bed – she had knocked on the wall for Aunt Phyllis. Aunt Phyllis had already sent for the doctor.

'But what's wrong?' I asked.

Dad moved his head quickly in a shaking movement as if trying to throw something off, then exclaimed, 'It's her stomach, there's something wrong with her stomach.'

I ran before him up the hill, and burst into the front room, to be greeted by Aunt Phyllis with the command, 'Be quiet! control yourself.'

When I stood by the bedside looking down at my mother, she seemed so much older that it could have been ten years since I last saw her instead of three hours. She did not speak but patted my hand twice; then my Aunt Phyllis moved me out of the room and followed me through to the kitchen, and there she said, 'Now you'll have to get your hand in. And not before time an' all. She'll have to be looked after. She should go to a hospital. But then she always thought she knew best. Now come along and get your things off and finish this washing. She was in the middle of it and it's a heavy one.'

As if in a dream, I took off my hat and coat and put on an apron. When I look back it seems I never took that apron off.

After two weeks in bed my mother seemed brighter and talked of getting up, but she did not get up, not for many weeks. Every night before I went to bed she would pat me on the hand and say, 'The morrow I must put my best foot forward, I can't lie here for ever.'

But in the morning she was always very tired again.

Dad hardly ever left the house except to sign on and go to the allotment, and he would help me with the work, but was no good with the cooking, though he would offer advice, saying, 'Your ma did it like this.' Yet no matter how hard I tried to follow the way Mam did it I always seemed to use twice as much stuff, and the result would be nowhere near as nice as when she had made it.

The money did not go so far either, and this was worrying us all. Although my money was not coming in, Dad could get no more from the unemployment exchange because Ronnie was still working; and then, too, we not only missed my mother's few shillings, but all the odds and ends she brought down from Mrs. Durrant's.

Every day Aunt Phyllis came in and washed my mother and made her bed, and sometimes my mother would say, 'Oh, Phyllis, you shouldn't trouble, I can manage on my own.' But she never told her not to come. And, moreover, every day my Aunt Phyllis told me in some way how badly I was managing.

One day when she was passing through the kitchen as I was dishing up the dinner she cast her eyes down on the cabbage which was a bit watery, and said, 'If you give that a shove it'll float away.'

To her astonishment, and to mine also, our Ronnie, who was standing by the hearth, turned on her, exclaiming, 'Leave her alone, Aunt Phyllis, she's not me mam and she's doing her best.'

Aunt Phyllis, in the act of walking away, stopped in her tracks, turned slightly and looked at Ronnie, and such was the expression in her eyes that Ronnie's head dropped before it and he turned gauchely towards the fire again, while Aunt Phyllis muttered something under her breath which I could not catch. But what she made sure I did catch was her parting shot, for at the kitchen door she turned on me almost in a white fury and exclaimed, 'By! you'll have something to answer for.'

As the outer door banged I turned to Ronnie, the pan still in my hand. 'What in the name of goodness have I done now?' I asked. 'All because the cabbage is a bit watery. Oh, I'll squeeze it again.'

I was flouncing back into the scullery when he caught my arm and said soothingly, 'Take no notice of her. The cabbage is all right. That woman's mad, she should be locked up. There'll be trouble with her one day, you'll see.'

Don and Sam came in every day to inquire after my mother, yet Don never went through to the front room, he always stayed in the kitchen. But he never managed to get me alone, nor did he manage to meet me outside, for whatever shift he was on I arranged to go for the shopping when I knew he would be at the pit.

Sam would sit by my mother's bedside as long as he was allowed, until she would say, 'Well, Sam, you'd better be trottin',' or until he heard Aunt Phyllis yell, 'Sam! You Sam!' Often he would say to me, 'Can't I do anything for you, Christine, get coal in or anything?' And nearly always my answer was, 'No, Sam, thanks; Dad's got it.'

The doctor's visits were spaced more widely apart now, which made Dad angry and he exclaimed one day, 'He'd be on the bloody doorstep if he could get his seven and a tanner each time. He'll get his bill.' And then he ended, 'My God! it makes you wish there was a bloody war, for then there'd be no shortage of money. They'd be crying out for us then.'

The week before Christmas my mother came into the kitchen and it was a time of rejoicing. I felt so happy that I seemed to do everything right; even the pastry I made turned out light and fluffy, and this caused the first real laugh there had been in the house for months. The world seemed to be right again. Dad put up the chains, Mrs. Durrant sent mother a big parcel of food, and Mollie came to see me and told me that she had left the shop for she couldn't stand it without me.

I had been surprised to see Mollie at the door, and I had invited her in after whispering to her, 'Don't swear, will you?' and she hadn't sworn for half an hour. I saw that my mother liked her. Then Stinker came in and, wanting to be friendly, put his paws on her leg and tore her stocking. At this she exclaimed in dismay, 'Oh, you bugger! And me best pair.' Then giving a laugh she ended, 'That's another bloody one an' eleven gone down the drain – cost price, too.' She gave me a push. I glanced at my mother and saw that her face was surprised and straight, but Ronnie and Dad were almost convulsed.

Mollie soon took her departure, and Mam asked me, immediately the door had closed on her, 'Does she usually swear?'

'No, Mam,' I lied. I knew that my mother did not believe me.

Christmas over, Mam's energy seemed to flag again, and one day I found her crying and she said, 'Go down to Father Howard and ask him if he will kindly say a mass for me.' Then she drew her purse to her and, counting out five shillings in sixpences and coppers, added, 'You'd better take this with you. Offer it to him, but he may not take it.'

Her request sounded so ominous that I hurriedly put on my hat and coat and went out. There was a cold wind blowing but the coldness of my hands, feet and face could not in any way compare with the coldness I was feeling round my heart. My mother was very ill; she was getting up, but this did not hide the fact that she was very ill.

Even in the biting wind there were men lining each side of the bridge and they called out to me and asked how she was.

The nine o'clock mass was just finishing and I saw Father Howard in the vestry. I made my request and offered him the five shillings, which he took quite casually and laid it on a shelf as if it were of no account.

When I returned home, Mam said, 'Well?' She did not ask if he was going to say the mass for her but ended, 'Did he take it?' I nodded silently and she said somewhat bitterly, 'My God!'

From this time on I started to go to mass every morning, even when there might be a chance of Don waylaying me. I went to Our Lady's altar after each service and begged her to spare my mother. And she answered my prayers, for in the months that followed my mother gradually regained her strength and, though she could not lift anything heavy or do housework, she resumed the cooking and became something of her former self. . . .

Then it was my birthday, 26th April. For my birthday present my mother had made me a coat. She had unpicked and turned a coat that Mrs. Durrant had sent down and had passed the hours, when she had to keep her feet up, by sewing the whole of it by hand. It was a beautiful coat, tight at the waist and full in the skirt, and I could not wait to get it on. Our Ronnie bought me a scarf, and Sam, who never had any money except for the odd copper my mother slipped him, carved my name with a penknife on a round piece of oak, with holes pierced in it so that it could be hung up like a picture. I was delighted with his present, and my pleasure pleased him greatly I could see. Don bought me nothing, and that also pleased me, for I did not want to have to thank him for anything, although during the last few months he had said nothing to me that anyone else could not have heard. Aunt Phyllis, Don and Sam were invited to tea. My Aunt Phyllis refused on some pretext or other, but Don and Sam came, and as we all stood in the kitchen looking at the lovely spread my mother had managed to make, Don moved to where his mack was lying on the head of the couch and from under it he brought a parcel, and, coming to me, put it into my hands, saying, 'Here's your birthday present.'

I tried to smile and mumbled some words of thanks. And then he said, 'Well, aren't you going to open it?'

My mother had not spoken, but she took the scissors from where they hung on a nail at the side of the mantelpiece and handed them to me. I cut the string and opened the parcel to reveal a green leather case. It was in the shape of an oblong box, and when I lifted the lid my eyes popped in amazement. It was a dressing-case, complete with bottles and jars, and the inside of the lid was fitted with glass to form a mirror. There was even a little case which held a manicure set.

I raised my eyes from the gift and looked at him and said, 'Thanks, but – I can't take it.'

He turned away and sat down at the table, saying, 'Don't be silly.'

My mother and Dad were standing one on each side of me now looking down into the box, and my mother said clearly, 'This must have cost a pretty penny, Don.'

'Aye, I'm not saying it didn't. Nobody's arguin' about it. Are we going to start eating, Aunt Annie?'

'Christine's not used to gifts like these. ...' My mother stopped and everybody moved uneasily. Embarrassment filled the room.

We all came under it except Don who, swinging round in his chair, faced my mother, saying, 'Look, Aunt Annie, I didn't steal the money, I worked for it. I've got a job on the side. She needn't be ashamed to take it.'

'What's this job you've got on the side, Don?' asked Dad quietly, as he took his seat at the table and motioned us all to be seated.

'Selling things, Uncle Bill,' said Don. 'I do odd things for Remmy, the second-hand dealer, you know, I sell things for him.'

'What kind of things?' Dad was not looking at him but at my mother as he took a cup from her.

'Oh all kinds, junk and such. There's a car in at present. I wouldn't mind going in for it meself. He only wants twenty quid for it.'

'Put that down,' said my mother quietly.

I was still standing with the dressing-case in my hands. 'But, Mam ...'

'Put it down. We'll talk about it later.'

As I sat down at the table Don, looking at me, exclaimed with a laugh, 'I didn't buy it to 'tice you to make up, your skin's fine as it is, isn't it, Aunt Annie?'

My mother was still pouring out the tea and she did not look at Don as she answered, 'Yes, it's quite all right as it is.'

My birthday tea that had promised to be a joyful occasion turned out to be only a stiff, rather ceremonious one, where everybody said 'Thank you' and 'No, thank you' and nobody laughed much except Don.

Our Ronnie, I saw, was furious, and after tea, as we all sat round the fire, I could not bear the stiffness in the atmosphere any longer, and so I said to him 'What about that funny rhyme you made up about Miss Spiers. Go on, read it.' I turned to my mother. 'It's funny, Mam,' I said. Then again turning to Ronnie, I urged, 'Go on, read it. You said you would after tea.'

'Yes, go on,' said my mother.

Somewhat mollified, Ronnie pulled from his pocket a piece of paper and, glancing self-consciously around the room, said, 'It's called "The Prayer of Mary Ellen Spiers".' Then he gave a little laughing 'Huh!' before he began:

> O Lord, she said, look after me
> And don't make me like the likes of she,
> Who, next door, in dark sin abounds
> A lipstick, rouge and film hound.
>
> O Lord, I beg, look after me
> Who only ever imbibes tea;
> Not like others with drops of gin,
> Which is the stimulant of sin.
>
> O Lord, I beg, take care of me
> From all those men who go to sea;
> Shield me, I pray, from their winks,
> And don't blame me, Lord, for what I thinks;
>
> And from those men who swarm the air,
> Fair bait I am for them up there.
> If I am not to become a flyer
> Work overtime, Lord, on . . .
>   MARY ELLEN SPIERS.
>
> From actors, Lord, protect me proper,
> Or else I'll surely come a cropper;
> Keep my dreams all dull and void,
> And lock the door, Lord . . . on Charles Boyd.
>
> Let me not mix, Lord, I pray,
> With poets and writers of the day;
> Keep my hands from their craft,
> And stop me, Lord, from going daft.
>
> And when I die, O Lord, remember
> My life has been one grey December;

I ain't never had men, wine or beer,
And, O Lord, ain't I bored down here.

Don, Sam and Dad were roaring before he had reached the last verse, and even Mam was making a vain effort to hide her amusement, but she admonished him, 'You shouldn't write things like that, 'tisn't right. Poor Miss Spiers.'

'Oh, Mam, it's only fun.'

'Poor woman,' said Mam again; then she turned to Sam and said brightly, 'Come on, Sam, sing us a song.'

Sam was nearly fourteen. He was growing but still had a shy reticence about him, and now he put his two hands between his knees and rocked his shoulders from side to side as he protested, 'Eeh! no, Aunt Annie, I can't sing properly.'

'You've got a lovely voice, lad. Come on, sing something. That one you were humming the other day.'

He turned his head sideways and glanced up at her, asking shyly, 'Which one was that?'

'Oh, I don't know. It went like this.' She hummed one or two bars, and he said, 'Aw, you mean "You May Not be an Angel"?'

'Aye, I suppose that's it. Come on now, on your feet.'

Lumbering from his chair, he turned it round and, holding the back for support, he began to sing. His voice was clear and true and pulled at something inside of me.

The song finished; we clapped and clapped, that is, all except Don, and he, laughing, said, 'He's got a cissie voice.'

'Nothing of the sort,' said my mother sharply, 'he's got a beautiful voice, a tenor voice. Sing again, sing something else, Sam.'

Sam shook his head and was about to resume his seat when I put in, 'Go on, Sam, sing another. Sing that one I like, "I'm Painting the Clouds with Sunshine".'

He looked at me and said, 'I don't know all the words of that one but I'll sing, "That's My Weakness Now", eh?'

The title and his shy look struck us all as very funny and once again the kitchen was ringing with laughter, and when he began, he himself could hardly get the words out for laughing. The tears were running down his cheeks, and as I looked at him I thought, Thanks, Sam, for he more than anyone else had made my birthday party.

77

Later, when Don and Sam had gone in next door, the dressing-case remained on the sideboard and we had a discussion about it as we sat round the fire.

'There's nothing much you can do,' said Dad, 'without causing trouble.'

'But I don't want her to have it,' said my mother.

'And,' I put in, 'I don't want it either.'

'Give it back to him,' said Ronnie, angered again at the thought of the present, and though Dad was for letting things rest as they were, he said, 'But that's the finish, mind, you'll take nothing from him again.'

'I won't use it,' I said; 'it's there for him when he wants it.' But later, when I took the case upstairs and looked at it under the light of the candle, I thought, 'Oh, if only I could use it.' It was so beautiful. If only Dad or Mam or Ronnie had bought it for me ... or Sam. Sam who never had a penny.

I went to bed and, strangely, it was of Sam I lay thinking, Sam and his nice voice. He would be leaving school this summer and he wanted to get a job on a farm if he could. There was little prospect of that hereabouts, but he had said to my mother he wouldn't mind going away, although, he had added, he would miss us all very much. Sam was nice. Thinking of him brought no conflict to my mind, not like when I thought of Don or even our Ronnie.

I don't know how long I had been asleep before I heard Ronnie's voice saying, 'Christine, I want to talk to you.' He hadn't come to my room for months. I thought he had got over all that silliness of wanting to talk to me in the night, but now he was whispering, 'Christine ... Christine.'

'What is it?' I said.

I was sitting up hugging the clothes around me, and he repeated, 'I want to talk to you.' He put his hand out to me, but I pressed away from him. I could see his face, for the night was light; it was white and his eyes were shining darkly.

'Don't use that case, will you?'

'Of course I won't, I've said so. Why did you wake me up for that?'

Screwing about on his hunkers he bent nearer to me, saying, 'I could kill him when he makes up to you like that. You don't want him, do you?'

'No, I've told you. And look, our Ronnie,' I exclaimed in

low rapid tones, 'if Mam or Dad knew you came in here there would be something to do, I'm telling you.'

'Why?' His voice sounded huffed.

'Don't keep saying "Why?" You know you shouldn't be ...'

'What harm am I doing, anyway?' he put in. 'I just want to talk to you.'

'But what about?' My voice sounded as desperate as I felt.

'Oh, heaps of things. I can't talk to anybody else, and we should be able to talk now. I want to talk about all kinds of things. Us, for instance – yes us, and ... and God ... man, the world, the devil, and the flesh.'

I knew that in the last bit he was quoting Father Howard's Sunday sermon, but as he said 'flesh' his hands came on to me and his voice changed to a sort of trembling groan as he whispered, 'Move over and let me sit near you, just on the top ... just on the top.'

'No, no!' I pressed myself against the wall; then springing up and on to my knees and holding the quilt in front of me, I gasped, 'Get out, our Ronnie; if you don't I'll yell for me mam.'

Slowly he drew himself up from his hunkers, and with his hands outstretched he began to plead, 'Christine ... Christine, honest to God, I meant nothing. I just wanted to sit against you. Honest.'

'Go. Go on ... get out!'

'You've got to believe me. Look, I won't ever touch you again. I just want to be with you and talk to you. Can't you see?'

'Go on. If you don't I'll shout. I will, mind. And if you come in again I'll tell me mam. Go on.'

His face took on such a look of sadness that I almost felt sorry for my attitude, but when the door closed on him I flew to it and jambed a chair under the knob, then rushing back into bed I covered my head with the bedclothes and prayed, 'Holy Mary, Mother of God, pray for us sinners, now and at the hour of our death, amen. Holy Mary, oh please, please don't let our Ronnie come in again, don't make me have to tell me mam. Oh please! please!'

Next morning I went to mass and to the side altar, and there I implored Our Lady to protect me. Against what I did not

79

say, I just asked her to keep me a good girl, to keep my thoughts and mind pure and never to let me do anything wrong.

Just when I passed over the bridge before ascending the hill I met Don. He stood dead in front of me, searching my face in an exaggerated fashion, then exclaimed, 'No makeup? Mam's forbidden it, eh?'

I felt very tired and somehow unable to do battle with him. Instinctively, I knew I had to fight the same battle against him as I had against Ronnie, and the thought, for the moment, had ceased to be terrifying and was just a dead weight on my mind. Quietly I replied, 'I'm not old enough for make-up; I'll use it some time.'

'Well, don't wait too long. By the way, I'm coming in to see your mam and dad shortly.'

I raised my eyes just the slightest. The house was always open to him, why should he make a statement like this?

Then he said, 'Any idea what I'll be after?'

I shook my head. 'No, none.'

'Now, now, don't be coy, the come-hither stuff doesn't suit you, Christine. You want me to put it into words? All right, I'll tell you. I'm going to say "Uncle Bill and Aunt Annie". I'm going to do it proper like, I'm going to say to them' – he now struck a pose before going on – ' "Will it meet with your approval that I take your daughter out, courtin' like?" '

My heart was pounding now and I said, tersely, 'You can save yourself the trouble, Don, and you know it. I thought we had finished with all that.'

The laughter slid from his face and his big mouth seemed to shrink until it looked like Aunt Phyllis's. Then he said quietly, 'I've behaved meself, I've kept me temper, I've done everything according to the book and even that doesn't suit you. Well, I'll do as I said. I'll ask, and if they don't approve then I'll do it in me own way ... the courtin', I mean. So make up your mind you're for me, Christine. I've always known it, and I'd put you in the river afore I'd let anyone else lay eyes on you.'

Under his fixed stare and his words, which were bringing a feeling of terror spurting up in me, I stood as if hypnotized, until a snuffling and a joyous yelp at my legs told me that Stinker had come to meet me, and I turned to him as to some kind, normal human creature and, heedless of my good coat, I stooped down and gathered his warm wriggling body up into my arms. As Stinker's tongue licked his welcome on my face I thought of what my mother had said, 'Don't show him you're afraid,' but I was afraid, and he knew it. It was impossible to feel as I did inside and it not to show in my eyes, but with an effort I brought out, 'You're mad, Don Dowling, quite mad.'

His next words made me more terrified than ever, for he said quite calmly, 'Yes I am, Christine, you're right there. I am mad where you're concerned. I'm stark, staring mad. I think I always have been.' Then putting out his hand he pushed Stinker's head roughly aside away from my face, and his tone had altered when he said, 'Don't let him lick your face like that, I can't stand it.'

'Leave him alone!' Suddenly I was angry, and because I was angry I had courage. 'Who cares what you can stand and what you can't stand? You're nothing but a big bully, Don Dowling. And don't you push him like that. And don't speak to me again.'

I marched away and he made no effort to stop me, but I knew he was watching me. As I neared the house my steps became slower and I put Stinker down. My courage had ebbed and fear was flowing over me again and I wanted to be sick.

When I got in my mother asked if anything was wrong and I said no, I was just cold. And I was cold, I was cold all through. I went upstairs and peered into the little square of mirror and my reflection brought me no comfort. I wished I looked like Mollie. At that moment I longed to be all Mollie, fat, merry and comfortable. As I stared at myself I got a sort of insight into my character and I knew that although I looked bonny, inside I was ordinary, and somehow I knew that my main desire was to remain so. I wanted to feel comfortable and easy, I wanted my days to be without turmoil or stress. Perhaps I would have taken a different attitude, a pride in my looks, if I had not been vitally aware that it was these very looks that aroused that something, that terrifying something, in both our Ronnie and Don.

Three days later Stinker was missing. At times he would go on the rampage, but whatever time of the year it was, the approach of darkness would find him at the back door. But this particular night there was no scratching or barking, and when nine o'clock came and he had not returned, Dad put his coat on and went on to the fells calling for him. He would not let me go with him. He was out for almost an hour, and when he returned he asked, 'Is he in yet?'

I shook my head.

Next morning I was up at dawn searching the woods. My steps seemed to be directed towards the tree bay, and when I reached it I almost vomited my relief. There was no tortured body nailed to the tree this morning.

I returned home relieved yet crying, and Dad said he would go down to the pound and see if anyone had picked him up as a stray and taken him there. When he returned, it was to say that Stinker was not in the pound.

That afternoon when Sam came out of school we searched the fells together, looking over crags and down narrow, shallow crevices near which we used to play when he was a puppy. And lastly the river, perhaps someone had pushed him in the river. What a silly thought, he could swim like a duck. As I plodded up from the river bank to the house again, Sam walking silently by my side, I was overwhelmed by a sense of loss. I had not really realized before that Stinker was not just our dog, he was my dog. The lads could call him until they were hoarse, but he would never obey them unless I gave him the word, and his greatest joy was when he could sneak upstairs and curl up on my bed. He did not manage this often as Mam did not believe in dogs lying on beds.

When he could not be found my thoughts turned to Fitty Gunthorpe and the maimed rabbit and the plucked bird. The two poor things seemed now to link up with Stinker and I cried and shuddered alternately. Then Fitty Gunthorpe faded into the back of my mind and into his place came Don, and this for no other reason than my remembering his rough handling of Stinker the other morning and my reaction to it. Unreasonably, I began to say, 'He's done something just to spite me. It's him . . . I know it's him.'

Then on the Thursday night I had to revise all my ideas and for the only time in my life I wanted to shower my gratitude on Don Dowling. So grateful was I that I almost threw myself at him and put my arms round his neck and kissed him, for he came up the backyard shouting, 'Christine!

Christine! look what I've got.' And there, on a lead of string, was Stinker, a rather thinner Stinker, but Stinker.

Down on my knees on the scullery floor I kissed and patted and hugged his shaggy head to me, and he wriggled his body all over me in joy at our meeting. Then I cast grateful eyes upwards to Don as my mother asked, 'Where on earth did you get him, Don?'

He was scratching the back of his head and looking down at Stinker and me as he replied, 'Just a mere piece of luck, Aunt Annie. I happened to go through Spillers Cut, you know where the taggerine yard is, and I heard a yelp, and something about it reminded me of this scallywag here. So I went in and put my head round the door of the shed, and there he was, tied up in what had been a horse-box. He nearly pulled a partition down when he saw me. The taggerine bloke said he had come in with some kids a couple of days before. He said he had left them all playing together in the yard and when he came back they were gone and the dog was tied up. He was waiting for them comin' back to claim him. He had fed him what he could, he said.'

'Oh, Don.' My gratitude was in my voice and eyes as I slowly stood up and said, 'Thanks. Oh, thanks.' I was about to add, 'I'm sorry I was so nasty,' but checked myself in time. Yet at this moment I was sorry, I found I was even liking him a bit.

He smiled down at me, saying, 'I thought it would put you on top of the world again having him back. You've been going round like an accident looking for an ambulance.'

I laughed shakily. 'I felt like one, too.' Then because his eyes were on me, I lifted Stinker up into my arms and went into the kitchen.

Life seemed a little more tranquil after this event. Don was nicer, our Ronnie left me alone at night, my mother continued to improve, at least I thought so. In fact she led me to believe that she was very much better because she said to me one day, 'You'll soon be able to go back to your job, lass.' Yet she gave no time limit. But I was in no hurry to return to Mrs. Turnbull's.

It had been a wonderful day for washing. I had got up early and had the washing done and everything dried and damped down ready for ironing by tea-time, and this had pleased her and she said, 'By, lass, you'll make a grand housewife before you're finished.' Then suddenly changing her tone she added, 'But I don't want you to have this kind of life. You've been made for something different besides washing. When you get married I hope you'll have one of them washing machines and a Hoover for the mats.' Suddenly her laugh was joined to mine and she said, 'Well, I know I'm daft. If you have a Hoover you won't have clippie mats, will you, you'll have carpets.' She nodded and ended, 'Aye, you'll have carpets, you'll have a house with carpets, all right.'

It was a lovely prophecy, and it made me feel happy.

She was sitting in her chair by the open door, her knitting in her hands, and she said in a tone that was warmly conspiratorial, 'What about having a cup of tea afore they come in, eh?' I nodded. One of the luxuries of her life was a cup of tea and a piece of fruit cake.

I had just mashed the tea and put the pot on the hob when I heard Aunt Phyllis's voice coming through the wall, and to it was joined Don's. They both seemed to be yelling, but not at each other. Going swiftly into the scullery where Mam, her hands pressed tightly into her lap now, was straining her ear towards the backyard, I whispered rapidly, 'They're on at Sam again, Mam. What's he done now I wonder?'

Mam shook her head, then whispered back, 'He's just this minute got in from school.'

We had not long to wait before we knew the trouble. While Dad was in the scullery washing his hands Sam came creeping in from the back door. His eyes were red and his face was swollen with crying. He did not look at my mother or me but went straight to Dad and, rubbing his finger along the outside of the tin dish in which Dad was washing, he fixed his gaze on the muddy water and said almost in a mumble, 'Uncle Bill, they're going to make me go to the pit.'

Dad reached out for the towel, then asked, 'When's all this come about?'

'Just the day,' said Sam.

'Did you tell them you wanted to go to a farm somewhere?'

'Aye. Yes, I've been on about it all the time, but our Don came in the day and said he spoke for me up top.'

84

Sam was still looking at the water and still moving his finger back and forth on the outside of the dish, and Dad looked down at him for a moment before turning away and saying, 'Well, you'll have to look at it this way, Sam. Jobs are as scarce as gold dust. Some would say you're very lucky to get a chance of a start, although I did hear' – now he turned and looked at my mother – 'I did hear they're signing some men on again.'

My mother took her interest from Sam and said eagerly, 'They are?'

'Aye, not here but further afield, but it's a good sign. I'm going down first thing in the morning to have a talk with Lambert and see if there will be any chance.' He looked up at the ceiling and exclaimed, 'It'll be funny going down again, like starting a new life.'

I looked from Dad to Sam. Sam's head had drooped lower, he was no longer looking at the water but down to the floor. I went to him and put my arm round his shoulders, and Dad's attention was drawn to him again and he punched him playfully on the head saying, 'It's not really bad, Sam, you get used to it. You won't believe it, but I felt the same as you when I started. Thirteen I was and couldn't sleep for nights.'

'But, Uncle Bill, I'm . . . I'm . . .' The tears were in Sam's eyes again as he looked at Dad and he could not bring himself to say, 'I'm frightened of the dark,' but we all knew what he meant.

'Come and have some tea.' It was my mother speaking now. 'I've got some lardy cake.'

After tea Sam stayed in our kitchen until Aunt Phyllis's voice yelled from the backyard, 'You, Sam!' and when he was gone my mother said, 'Poor little beggar, and him scared without a light.' Then getting up from her chair and pushing the seat level under the table, she said, 'That's that Don.'

Neither Dad nor I made any comment.

Later that evening I found it impossible to sit quietly with my mother and so went upstairs, then came down again and walked from the front-room window to the kitchen window. The house felt airless and I had a sudden longing for a sight of the river. 'Do you mind if I take a walk, Mam?' I said.

'No,' she said hastily, 'You look peeky. It's this heat. Where do you think of going?'

'Just down to the river,' I said.

'You wouldn't like your dad to come with you?'

'No, no,' I shook my head quickly.

'Then go out the front way,' she said.

This was so that Don, if he was in the kitchen or in his room which looked on to the back as mine did, would not see me making for the river.

I did not even go upstairs to tidy my hair, I just slipped off my apron and went quickly out of the front door. I walked sedately down the street, around the corner and on to the fells proper. But once I was hidden behind the rise of the land I began to run and did not stop until I had reached the river bank, and there, looking down into the water, I kept drawing in deep gulps of air. Then I decided to go along the river as far as the bend. It seemed years since I had been to the big bend. The river was all bends but the big bend was where it turned sharply and rounded the foot of Brampton Hill. It was a good two-mile walk from where I was now, but it was not yet twilight and I knew I could do it and be back before dark.

I decided to cross by the stepping-stones further along and walk on the other bank. The path there was mostly clear, and it was prettier than on this side.

When I came to the stones I saw a couple with their arms around each other. They were both standing on the same stone. It was not very big and would hardly hold them, but they clung together laughing at the water rushing noisily round their feet. When the girl turned her face towards me I saw that I knew her. Her name was Edna Stace and she had been in my class. She and her boy friend made for the bank, and I said, 'Hullo, Edna,' and she said, 'Hullo, Christine.' That was all.

Jumping quickly from one stone to the other, I hurriedly crossed the river, and when I stepped on to the far side I did not look back at them but went on, feeling somewhat embarrassed and strangely very lonely. It was a feeling I had not experienced before. It was as if there was nobody in the world who loved me, and as I walked I thought, 'Fancy Edna having a lad.'

Later on I passed two men fishing and an elderly couple out for a walk, then I saw no one else until I reached the big bend. It was lovely at the big bend. The river was wider here and had not the tumbling turbulence of the narrower stretches, and rising steeply from the other side was Brampton Hill, the side of it that few people saw, and on the top of the hill there were railings, and inside the railings were trees. These were the grounds of some of the big houses of Brampton Hill. I could see from where I stood that there were gates let in to some of the railings and pathways leading down to the river. I sat down and rested on the bank for a while and, looking up towards the houses I couldn't see, I wondered what it would be like to live in one of them with a garden that bordered on the river. Well, didn't our houses almost border on to the river? But those railings with the gates in them spoke of something different from Fenwick Houses.

As I sat a mist came from nowhere and began to spread itself evenly over the water, like butter under a hot knife. It covered the river and I rose to my feet knowing that the heat of the day was over and soon it would turn surprisingly cold. I walked much quicker going back and had almost reached the stones again when I saw, crossing them, a young man. In the first glimpse I recognized him. He wasn't wearing a scarf this time, but it was one of the two young men who had watched Ronnie, Don and me running down the hill the night we went to the social. He stepped off the last stone as I reached the bank and we looked at each other. He looked the same as I remembered him, pale-faced, with dark eyes almost black in this light. And as he looked at me he did not blink and my eyes fell before his gaze. And then he spoke. 'Good evening,' he said. It was strange but I found myself stammering as I replied, 'Good evening.' Then although I had no intention of running I almost leaped across the stones, and when I got to the other side I had to take a firm hold of myself to stop myself from scampering away like a rabbit. 'Don't be silly,' I said, 'he'll think you're daft.'

I did not look across the river but I knew for certain that he was standing watching me, and so I walked as sedately as possible, with my head up and my arms swinging just a little. I had to stop my legs from striding out for, being long, they inclined to big steps.

I kept up my sedate walk until I rounded the first bend, because from here he could not see me. Then I almost jumped as I glanced across the river, for there he was walking nearly

87

parallel with me on the other side. He smiled and caught my glance. But I did not smile back, I kept looking straight ahead, and even when I came to the bank below our houses I did not look across but turned up the hill. And when I reached the top my heart was beating rapidly. But, strangely, I did not feel lonely any more.

People were sitting on their doorsteps getting the cool evening air and they said, 'Hullo, Christine. By, it's hot isn't it?' 'Yes,' I said, 'it is.' I found speaking difficult, for my throat seemed tight.

'Where did you go?' asked my mother.

'The big bend,' I replied.

'All that way?' she said. 'Aren't you tired after that washing the day?'

I shook my head. I had never felt less tired in my life; my body was afloat, my heart was now leaping and bouncing within me; all I wanted to do was to get upstairs into my room and into bed and think and think.

When at last I found myself between the sheets I buried my head in the pillow, and in the deep darkness his face came up clearly outlined. He was beautiful . . . lovely, and I had not only seen him twice, I had been seeing him for years, for his was the face around which I had dreamed my budding dreams. That night going down the hill, I thought I had seen him before, and now I knew that in some strange way he had always been familiar to me. Turning on my back I lay staring out through the window to the star-laden sky. He was under that sky and somewhere quite near, and he was thinking of me. I knew he was thinking of me. That last look had told me that he would think of me all night and all tomorrow.

I sat quickly up in bed. Tomorrow night I would walk to the big bend again, and if he spoke I wouldn't be silly, I would speak back. But tomorrow night was eons of time away – I couldn't see how I was going to live until tomorrow night. . . .

Tomorrow night came after a day of ironing and doing bedrooms. The day had been much cooler, and by half past six the sun had gone in and it was not such a nice evening. Then after the meal was over and I had washed up and trying to keep all excitement from my voice, I said, 'I'm going for a short walk, Mam.'

She raised her eyes from her patching and said, 'All right, lass.'

Ronnie was sitting by the table and he had lifted his head quickly when I spoke, and I thought for a terrible moment he would say he was coming with me, but to my relief he did not. He dropped his eyes to his book again. He was always reading, always getting books from the library, but since the night I told him to get out of my room he had not talked to me as he used to, and was short with me – sometimes he wouldn't look at me for days.

I slipped on my coat and went out, and when I reached the end of the street I stopped myself from running – I must walk sedately, he could be anywhere on the river bank. Then my walk was halted. What if he wasn't there? I felt sick and my steps became slower as I neared the river.

As far as I could see along both banks I was the only one out for a walk. I continued up to the stones, across them and along the far bank. I stood as I had last night looking up at the gardens across the river. Once again I saw the mist come over the water, and tonight it brought an immediate chill, and the chill was on my heart, too. Slowly, very slowly, I walked back to the stepping stones. I crossed them and made my way along the other bank and did not see a soul until I was nearly below our houses, and then across the meadow on the other side came the black-coated figure of Father Ellis. In my present state of acute disappointment I did not want to speak even to Father Ellis, but he had recognized me over the distance and waved to me, so I waited until he reached the far bank and then we shouted over to each other.

'How are you, Christine?' he called.

'All right, Father,' I called back. I was not all right, I felt I would never be all right again.

'I'll be over one day next week.'

'Oh good, Father, Mam will be pleased.' Father Ellis was not on our district now, but he visited us at odd times. Since that Sunday when Father Howard had delivered his notable sermon on morality the two young priests had been moved from district to district. About every month there was a change round, and it was whispered that things were not happy in the presbytery.

'Hasn't it been hot?'

'Yes, Father.'

'Is your mother any better?'

'Yes, Father, quite a bit.'

'Oh, that's good. I say a prayer for her every day.'

'Oh, thank you, Father.'

'You're growing tremendously, Christine. It's ages since we had a walk ... we must have a walk and a chat, like old times.'

'Yes, Father, yes.'

'Well, good-bye, Christine.'

'Good-bye, Father.'

He went away, waving his hand, and I turned up the hill from the river.

The next fortnight I walked back up the hill every night. Inside I felt sad and lost and lonely, and my mother thought I was sickening for something. 'You're doing too much,' she would say; 'this kind of work is too heavy for you. All that washing. You weren't cut out for it.' I looked at her and smiled and asked, 'What about you?' and she had replied, 'I'm different, lass.'

This answer made me feel more lonely still.

In the weeks that followed only two things of any note happened: Don Dowling got a car and Father Ellis lost his temper with our Ronnie. This latter happened on his promised visit. He saw a book on the dresser and he went and picked it up and, holding it up at arm's length, said, 'Who's reading this?'

Our Ronnie, coming out of the scullery buttoning up his shirt, said firmly, 'I am, Father.' The priest looked at him across the room for a moment, then at the book, and as he placed it back on the dresser I could see that he was making a great effort to be his jovial self as he said, 'Well, Ronnie, no offence meant, but I don't think you're ready for Martin Luther yet. The mind needs training before you read such things.'

'Why?'

Ronnie's question was snapped out, and in it was a challenge, and from that moment they began to argue, and when my mother interrupted and said, 'Enough of that!' Father Ellis raised his hand and said, 'No, Mrs. Winter, leave him alone, let him go on.'

I was setting the table and buttering the bread, and most of their talk was far above my understanding, but I remember being amazed that our Ronnie knew so much, and my attention was caught when he said, 'But we are told, Father, that Satan was a fallen angel, he had been cast out of heaven, yet we're told that heaven is the reward of good people. Can you explain how Satan ever got in? And is there a power which can turn good people into bad in heaven?'

As Father Ellis was about to reply, Ronnie, with what was to me awful temerity, put in quickly, 'And you say God didn't create evil, but we are told that God created everything and there is nothing that wasn't created by him, then where does evil come in?'

Father Ellis's voice held real anger now as he replied, 'I can't answer your questions in a minute. It has taken scores of great men a lifetime to ponder them, but if you want to find the answer to these questions I'll help you. But there's no need for you to attack the Church and God Almighty himself because of your limited intellect.'

'Oh, Father, I'm sorry.' My mother was wringing her hands, and she looked threateningly at Ronnie as she said, 'When your dad comes in I'll have something to tell him.'

'There's no need, Mrs. Winter. We all go through these phases, but we don't get so angry about them, that's all.'

Father Ellis did not stay long, and when he had gone my mother, her hands in her lap, sat helplessly looking at Ronnie. And then she said, 'Well, lad, you've asked for a catastrophe the day.'

'Oh, Mam, for heaven's sake be your age. This is nineteen-thirty nine, you're not struck down dead the day if you talk back to a priest.'

He got up and marched out, and my mother turned and looked at me. I felt the same as she did: things happened when you went for a priest. My mother was very superstitious and she had handed it on to me: I never cut my nails on Friday, nor walked under a ladder at any time, and if there were knives crossed on the table I uncrossed them quickly and made the sign of the cross so that there would not be a row in the house; if a picture dropped, or we heard a cricket on the hearth we knew it was a sign of a death, and if one person died in the street two others would be sure to follow, so for days we waited for catastrophe to overtake us.

Then Don Dowling drove up to the front door in his car. It was an old one but it had been done up, and he tooted the horn so loudly that it brought the whole street out. Aunt Phyllis was at her door making no effort to hide her pride in her son, while my mother and I stood side by side on our step.

'I didn't know you could drive, Don,' said my mother.

'Oh, I've been practisin' for some time, Aunt Annie. Come on, get in. And you Ma.' He beckoned his mother.

But both Aunt Phyllis and my mother shook their heads. Next he turned to me saying, 'What about it?' But I backed a step into the passage, and gave a little laugh as I said, 'No, not me Don, I'm petrified of cars.'

He did not press me further. Then under the admiring gaze of the entire street he drove the car away, round the top corner, down the back lane and on to the main road again.

As we watched the car disappear down the hill my mother, feeling that the occasion required something of her, turned to Aunt Phyllis and said, 'By, he's getting on, isn't he?' And Aunt Phyllis replied, 'Yes, and nobody to thank but himself and his own brains. And this is only a beginning, he won't be much longer in the pits.'

My mother said nothing to this but turned indoors, and when we reached the kitchen she said to me, 'Now mind, Christine, don't you go out with him in that car.'

'As if I would,' I said. We looked at each other, then re-sumed our duties.

And so the days went on with a dull sameness, and I won-dered if this was going to be my life forever, and I began to long to get a job. And then I saw him again – the young man.

What made me open our front door at that moment I don't know. I was cleaning the room out. There was no need for me to open the door but I opened it to look out into the street, and there he was, walking towards me. He had a walking stick in his hand and was evidently making for the wood. One minute he was in the middle of the road, the next he was stand-ing on the pavement right opposite me, and I could not see his face for a silvery light that was floating before my eyes. But I heard his voice saying, 'Why, hallo.' And when I said 'Hallo' back, the mist cleared and I saw him.

'We meet again.'

I did not answer. Our eyes had not moved from each other's face.

'It's a beautiful day. I was going for a walk in the wood.'

'Oh,' I managed to say.

'Do you live here?'

I inclined my head.

He was going to speak again when my mother's voice came from within. She wasn't calling me, just carrying on the conversation where we had left off before I opened the door. His eyes moved from my face and looked behind me. Then he said in a low tone, 'Will you be walking by the river tonight?' I lowered my gaze and forced my voice to say, 'Yes, I'll be going that way.' 'Good-bye,' he said. 'Good-bye,' I replied. But he did not go, and it was I who made the first move. I turned about, took hold of the door and shyly closed it. Then stood with my back against it, my hands holding the front of my dress. My heart was racing, and not only my heart but every vein in my body was moving to a kind of throbbing pain. I could even feel the blood in my legs as it went down the veins.

I began to sing. I finished the room in a blissful daze, and my mother, putting her head round the door, said, 'By, you are painting the clouds with sunshine and no mistake. I've never heard you sing like that for a long time.'

At half past six I was on the river bank. There had been no time stated but he was there waiting for me, just below our houses at the spot where I used to plodge. He came forward quickly with no sign of embarrassment, no gaucheness or buttoning of coat, no shuffling of feet or fumbling with words. We stood for a moment looking at each other as we had done that morning, then he asked softly, 'What's your name?'

'Christine,' I said, 'Christine Winter.'

'Christine,' he repeated. 'It suits you. Mine is Martin Fonyère.'

His name had a foreign sound and I could only describe it to myself as Fon-year.

'Where would you like to go ... Christine?' My name sounded like music coming from his mouth. It had never been spoken like that before.

'Along the river bank.'

'Well,' he smiled, 'that won't cost much. And I admire your choice, it's a lovely walk.'

My body shaking, my feet all sixes and sevens, I stumbled over a tuft of grass before I had gone half a dozen paces, and when his hand came out and steadied me I wondered what he must think of me not being able to keep my balance on level ground. Once I was steady he took his hand away and did not touch me again until we were crossing the stepping stones, when his hand came naturally to my elbow as he guided me down on to the first stone. Then he took my hand and helped me over as if I had never crossed them before, and when we reached the other side I longed intensely for his fingers to remain on mine. But he released his hold and we walked side by side but not close.

By the time we reached the big bend not only my heart but all that was me was entirely lost to this creature, this wonderful creature. He was not a boy like either Don or our Ronnie, yet he was not much older, perhaps twenty. But in his talk he appeared more of a man than even my dad did.

Father Ellis was the only educated man I had ever talked to, but Father Ellis's fluency of speech and charm of manner were as candlelight to the sun when compared to – to Martin's. I found his name dancing through my head, shutting out even the remarks he was making.

We were standing on the bank looking up at the gardens of Brampton Hill when his voice recalled me sharply to him. He was laughing as he said, 'What are you dreaming about?'

I wanted to say, 'You and your name,' but I only looked at him and returned his laugh.

'Do you often dream?'

Again I wanted to say, 'I always dream when I'm happy,' but what I said was, 'I haven't much time to dream.'

'Tell me about yourself.'

It came so easy for me to tell him, not about myself, for there was nothing to tell, but about my mother and Dad and our Ronnie. I did not mention the Dowlings. When I finished he did not make any comment, nor did he tell me about his life, only that he was staying with friends on Brampton Hill and that he had just finished at Oxford.

The long twilight came and the mist floated around us as

we walked back in the gathering dust, and I cannot remember what we talked about, but when we reached the bank below the houses he caught hold of my hand and said urgently and in a different tone from that which he had used all evening, for now it was so intimate it caught at my breath and held it, 'Don't go yet, Christine.' Our faces were close, our eyes drawing something trembling from the other's. I swallowed deeply and murmured, 'I . . . I can't. I must go, they'll be waiting for me. My brother may come down to look for me.'

His grip on my hand tightened and he asked, 'When can I see you again?'

'Tomorrow,' I whispered. 'I could get out at six.'

At this he frowned slightly, then said, 'I'm committed for tomorrow evening, most of the time anyway.' Then pressing my hand even tighter he added, 'But I'll try to make it, although if I'm not here by seven o'clock don't wait. But I'll be here without fail on Sunday night, sixish. All right?'

Our faces remained stationary, then his eyes dropped to my lips and I felt a heat passing over my body.

'I . . . I must go.'

'Good night, Christine.'

As I backed away from him he still held on to my hand.

'Good night, Martin,' I whispered. Then with a little tug I released myself and, forgetting to be sedate, I ran up the hill, and I had to resist the temptation of flinging my arms around myself and leaping into the air for the old ecstatic feeling was in me as never before.

As I came to the corner of the street I ran into Sam and something in his eyes brought me to a halt. 'What is it, Sam?' I asked, smiling my happiness down on him. He dropped his head and moved his toe in the dirt of the road, before he asked, 'Who's the lad, Christine?'

My heart missed a beat, and in the space there rushed in thoughts of our Ronnie and Don, and just for a second I was filled with dread; I remembered Ted Farrel.

I bent towards him and pleaded, 'Sam, don't say anything, will you, not about me being up the river with anyone?'

He lifted his eyes to mine and said, 'No, Christine, I won't say anything.'

'Promise?'

'Aye, of course I do.'

I touched his hair lightly with my hand before going on up the street and into the house singing not, 'I'm Painting the Clouds with Sunshine' ... but, 'Oh! tomorrow, tomorrow, tomorrow; oh! Martin, Martin, Martin.'

Saturday started hot. By noon the heat was almost unbearable, everybody was saying it was the worst yet, as if the heat was a form of epidemic.

I was preparing a salad when Don came into the scullery. He was all dressed up and he said in a quiet, even nice voice, 'Will you come for a run to Whitley Bay the night?'

'Thanks, Don,' I answered quite pleasantly, 'but I can't leave me mam.'

His face darkened just the slightest and he said, 'What, not for an hour? I'll ask her.'

'No.' I put my hand on his sleeve, and the pleasantness went out of my voice now as I stated flatly but firmly, 'It wouldn't be any use, I wouldn't go anyway.'

His whole attitude changed in a flash and he stood looking at me and grinding his teeth together until I heard the crunching. Then he growled, 'You won't have the decent way, will you? You always make me get on the raw, don't you? It seems to give you a kick.'

'Don't be silly,' I said.

'Silly, am I?'

'Yes, of course you are. I don't know what you mean ... on the raw.'

'You don't, eh? You're so innocent. Well, you will some day, and that's a promise.'

The door slammed and for once his threats did not leave me trembling and apprehensive.

Nothing could touch me today, no fear of Don Dowling or our Ronnie or anybody in the world. I bent down and rolled Stinker on to his back where he was sitting near the wash-house pot. We had a secret, Stinker and I, for last night I had smuggled him upstairs after Mam went to bed. I did not dare transcribe my need of him into thoughts, but deep down I knew I wanted to hold something.

Stinker lay in ecstatic calmness as I scratched his tummy, and my mother, coming into the kitchen, said, 'You'll have that beast as daft as yourself afore you're done.' She laughed, then asked soberly, 'What was he after?'

I went on scratching Stinker as I said offhandedly, 'Oh, the usual.'

'He never gives in,' said my mother. And she added, 'That frightens me.'

It usually frightened me, too, but today, like Stinker, I was experiencing ecstasy; it was an armour surrounding me.

Across the dinner table our Ronnie said, 'I'm going to Windy Nook to see a cricket match, you comin'?'

'No thanks,' I said; 'it's too hot to sit out all that time.'

I saw a shadow pass over his face, and he did not take his eyes off me as he added, 'You can sit in the shade.'

'I don't feel like it. I'm a bit tired and I've had enough of the heat without sitting out in it, shade or not.'

After he had left the house, stamping out without saying good-bye to anyone, Dad exclaimed, 'I don't know what's come over that lad lately. He never used to be short-tempered. It's all these fandangle books he reads, stuffing his head with things he can't understand. He'll find he's got enough to face in life without piling on the agony. But he can only live and learn like the rest of us.'

Around the middle of the afternoon the heat became unbearable, and it being Saturday and the house all cleaned and nothing more to do in the way of work except meals until Monday morning, my mother said she was going to have a lie down. And she added, 'Why don't you put yourself on the bed for half an hour and open a window wide. It'll be as cool up there as anywhere.'

I was sixteen and joy was throbbing in me and my mother was telling me to lie down – only women who were worn out with families and grinding housework ever went to lie down in the afternoon. When Mam saw the look on my face she gave a little laugh and said, 'Well, lass, you look so white and peaky. But no, I don't suppose you want to lie down.' Then, as if to afford me some pleasure, she ended, 'After tea we'll have a bath. We needn't put the pot on, just a few kettles. We'll have it afore Ronnie gets back.'

I made no comment. After tea I was going to the river.

When she had gone into the front room I did go upstairs. I stood by the window and looked down on the silver thread

97

of water twisting its way through the valley bottom. In just over three hours I would be on its bank with Martin – that's if he could get away. Oh, he must get away, he must. If I did not see him tonight I would die. I could not wait another day before seeing him. I put my arms round myself and hugged my joy and trepidation to me.

At six o'clock I was ready. I had changed all my clothes and was wearing a blue cotton dress with a square neckline, and on my face I had rubbed, for the first time, some cream from one of the jars in the dressing-case. The irony of using Don's 'sprat to catch a mackerel' to beautify myself for another boy did not strike me at the time. I only knew I wanted to smell nice. And I had tied my hair back with a ribbon, and now I was ready.

I was going for a walk, I told my mother. She nodded, and as I went to go out she said, 'And what is that nice smell you've got on you?'

'It's soap,' I lied, 'one of the tablets I got for Christmas.'

The heat had not lifted, and in the short time it took me to get to the river bank I felt sticky all over. He wasn't there. Well, it wasn't anywhere near seven o'clock yet. I'd walk a little way along the bank but keep myself in view from this spot. My heart was beating wildly, and at the same time I felt sick with apprehension in case he should not come.

I lost count of the times I walked that particular stretch of bank; and when the market clock struck seven I could actually have vomited in the river. There was still tomorrow night, I consoled myself, but tomorrow night was as years away – there was all tonight to get through. And tomorrow night the bank would be lined with couples; it always was on Sunday nights. Saturday night it was rarely you saw one couple or even a man fishing. Saturday night in Fellburn was picture night, or dance night, and the men who fished during the week usully went to the bars on a Saturday night; it was also a general club night. Tonight we would have had the river to ourselves, the world to ourselves. I wanted to see no one and hear no one but him, and he had not come.

I walked slowly up to the stepping stones, across them, and in a sauntering gait made my way to the big bend. By the time I reached it my hair was damp on my forehead, there were beads of moisture round my lips and my dress was sticking to my shoulder blades.

I sat down on the bank and looked at the water and there came over me a longing to drop into its inviting coolness, and this thought brought a faint resentment against my mother. Why had she not let me learn to swim? If I could swim I wouldn't have this sticky, awful feeling now. Then I chided myself strongly for daring to feel like this about Mam, Mam who was so good, so kind, so wonderful to me. I knew the reason now why she hadn't let me learn to swim, and knowing Don Dowling I should be grateful to her, and knowing our Ronnie, too, I should be grateful to her, although she knew nothing about that.

My eyes were drawn swiftly up from the water by the sound of laughter coming from a garden on top of the Hill. There was no one to be seen but I knew there were several people in that garden and I began to wonder what they were doing. Was he there? Was he laughing? I got to my feet and began the long walk home.

I passed one couple, they were sitting on the river bank and the boy was taking the girl's shoes off – they were going to plodge. This sight hurt me so much that I could have cried, and I had to tell myself not to be silly. What was wrong with me anyway? There was no answer to this.

As I came nearer home I was loath for my walk to come to an end. If I went into the house and he should come after all and not find me? The thought was agony. Then I came opposite the place where the lads used to bathe. There were the bushes where they had hung their clothes and the well-worn path they had made leading down to the river. On this side of the river there was also a wide clump of bush, but the river path skirted this. But now I noticed for the first time another path that went through the thicket and down to the water's edge, likely a fishermen's path, and just to give myself something to do to lengthen the walk I took this path. Within a few steps the walls of the shrubbery widened to form a small clearing with a number of grassy hillocks with the grass well worn in parts, and I guessed, with a blush at the thought, that this was where the courting couples came. They would be screened from both the river and the other pathway here.

The river seemed very low at this point, for below the bank there was about six feet of its bed showing in sand and gravel. It looked like a little beach and so inviting. Within a second I had slipped over the bank and was sitting on it. Here, much nearer to the water, the thought came again, Oh, if I could only swim. I imagined what it would be like to feel the water flowing over my body. Well I couldn't swim, but there was nothing to stop me plodging. This at the moment seemed a poor substitute, just something that bairns did and, at my age, something to be spurned, but, nevertheless, I took off my stockings and shoes and, lifting up my dress well above my knees, I walked slowly into the water. It was cool, smooth and soothing, and I went back and forward kicking my feet gently. It came just below my calves and the longing for the feel of it about my legs became so insistent that I was drawn further in. But I had no intention of going actually near the middle for that was where the deep part was. When the water was well above my knees the bottom was still visible, so I tucked my dress a bit further up and cautiously moved forward, making sure with each step that I could still see where I was going. When the water had almost reached my tucked-in dress, the bottom disappeared and I came to a sharp halt. There, with my feet on it, was the browny, golden washed shelf of rock on which I was standing, then, as if it had been sliced by a sharp knife, it ended abruptly and the water beyond looked black and forbidding. This was the deep part.

One minute I was looking down into it and the next my head was jerked upwards and joy raced through me as I heard a voice calling, 'Ooh . . . ooh! there.' He wasn't hailing me from the river bank but from half-way up the fell beyond. He must have come by the short cut over Top Fell. He had stopped and was waving, not with one hand but with two, and I answered in the same way. Throwing up my arms high above my head I waved them. I had forgotten for the moment where I was and in my joyous excitement I stepped forward. It seemed as if I jumped into the water feet first, and I heard myself screaming as I jumped. The water closed over my head and I sank swiftly into a cool green light, and I was swallowing this light in great gulps and it was choking me. My feet touched something hard which acted like a spring-board and I felt myself rising, and when my head broke through the surface after what seemed endless terrifying seconds, my arms and legs began to thrash wildly, and I spluttered and screamed before I went down again. Then once again I came up through the green lighted water, and now my panic told me that if I once more sank into that greenness it would be for good. And I did, but there was someone with me this time, holding me, pushing me, dragging me, turning me about. Never in my life had surprise been greater than when I found myself moving backwards through the water looking up at the sky. And when I was lying on my back on the little beach that I had left only minutes before, and bending over me was Martin, his hair flat on his head, his breath coming in great gasps and the water running down his bare body. Then the sky was blotted out and a blackness came over me and the next thing I remember was being on my face and water spurting from my mouth, and I was sick and Martin was holding my head. I felt humiliated and ashamed beyond all comprehension – that I should be sick in front of him.

'God, you gave me a fright. What made you go in when you can't swim?'

I wiped my mouth on the skirt of my sodden dress and shook my head slowly.

'How do you feel?'

'All right.'

He turned my face towards him and, looking into it, said, 'You don't look it. Turn round and lie still.'

I did as he bade me and as I turned over I noticed he was wearing bathing trunks. Before I could turn my glance away from them he touched his thigh and remarked casually, 'I was reckoning on having a dip later, but had to take it sooner than I anticipated.' He gave me a little smile, then added, 'I'm going across the river for my clothes. I won't be long. Lie still.'

I watched him walk into the water and with an effortless movement lie upon it, and in a moment or so he was rising out of it and going up the far bank. I saw him bundle his clothes together and tie them on his head with his belt. If I had not felt so limp and shaken I would have laughed at the sight of him swimming towards me.

When he came out of the water I pulled myself up into a

sitting position and watched him loosen his clothes and lay them on the bank. It was at this moment that a great shiver ran through my body and it brought him to my side.

'You're cold,' he said.

I shook my head.

'It's the shock. Look, take off that dress, it will dry on the bushes in no time, and put my coat round you.'

'Oh, no, no.'

He had made this preposterous suggestion so casually that my protest sounded silly even to myself, but even so I said I had better go home and get changed. He dropped on his knees at my side and his eyes compelled mine to look into them as he said softly, 'Don't go home, Christine. Take my coat. Go behind the bushes and take off your dress. It will dry in the sun in ten minutes, but you mustn't let it dry on you, you'll likely catch a chill that way.'

Without uttering one more word of protest I took his coat, and with his assistance climbed up the bank and went behind the bushes into the little clearing, and there, with a feeling that I was committing a great sin, I took off my dress and quickly slipped my arms into his coat, and not only buttoned it up but turned the collar up over my neck. Then in a small voice I said, 'Will you hang it up for me?'

He put his head over the bank and stretched out his hand and I handed him the dress. I was afraid to stand up, so I tucked my feet under the coat and clasped my knees with my hands. And when he said, 'Can I come up?' I answered, in a voice hardly above a whisper, 'Yes.'

He sat on the grass but not near me, and although I did not look at him I knew he was wearing his shirt. I began to part my hair with my fingers and wring the water from it, bending forward as I did this so that it would not wet his coat more than it had already done.

'Let me.' Although he was shy in the request his tone and manner took away from the proceedings any awkwardness that I might have felt. When he whipped off his shirt and began to dry my hair with it I wanted to make a protest, saying, 'Oh, it'll get wet,' but I didn't. I sat quiet as his hands rubbed my head gently back and forth. He was kneeling at my back and I could feel the warmth of his bare legs through the coat. The feeling of fright and exhaustion was passing and I was becoming consumed with a feeling of wonder, and I was aware for the first time that this feeling was wonder. I had experienced it in minute doses before: on that morning when I had taken my mother to see the first anemones in the wood, and the time I watched the sticky buds of the chestnut opening; and there was another time when, after having received communion, I had felt for one fleeting second that I held God within me. But these occasions had just been minute particles of a whole, and this was the whole. My body was warmed with it, glowing with it, and my heart was ready to burst with it, when he pulled my head back against him and, bending above me, looked down into my eyes. And I looked up into his. With a quick movement he was kneeling in front of me, his arms were about me and we were breathing into each other's faces. For one long second he held my look, then his lips were on mine, and the wonder burst from my heart. For the second time that evening I almost sank into oblivion, and for the second time I became afraid. For I was being kissed, really kissed, for the first time in my life, and I had no experience with which to judge the intensity of it. But I knew that I was a little frightened. With an effort I eased myself away, and once again we were looking at each other. And then he laughed, and, taking my hands in his, he pressed them to his chest and said, over and over again, 'Christine . . . Christine . . . Christine.' I found his voice as intoxicating as his kiss. Like a runner pausing for breath, he gasped as he flung himself down, and I was relieved for the moment of the bewitchment of his countenance as he pressed his face into my side.

'You know the first time I saw you?' His voice was muffled.

I nodded as I said, 'Yes, near the bridge.'

'You were with two friends, and I thought if ever I'd seen beauty and the beasts, this was it. You looked like something from another world, and I fell for you in that second. It was the last day of the Easter vac, and I cursed myself for having to go back. By the way, who were those two?'

My mouth was smiling as I said, 'My brother Ronnie, and Don Dowling. He lives next door.'

'Which was the big one? Your brother?'

'No, the other one.'

'I'm glad of that anyway. I hated them both on sight.' He

pressed my arm to him. 'But the big fellow, I remember, looked as if he would like to murder me.'

I found I was able to laugh at this, and I said, 'He likely did.'

He pulled my face round to him and demanded hotly, 'He wants you?' Then before I could make any answer, he said, 'Of course he does, he'd be a fool if he didn't. Do you know how beautiful you are, Christine?'

The reply on my lips was the usual one that I would give to any lad that had made such a statement, 'Don't be so silly,' but I never said it. I accepted the tribute gladly and smiled my thanks. I think, for the first time in my life, I was happy with what I was. Happy isn't the right word, in that moment of delight I was grateful for my face.

I still had my legs tucked up under the coat, and I was feeling stiff, and when I made a movement to ease the strain, he said, 'Stretch your legs out;' then laughed, 'I've seen legs before, you know.'

He made things so easy and natural, but still I found it embarrassing to look down the length of my bare legs. They looked very white and shocked me somewhat, and this set my thoughts working. But although I was conscious of what they were saying I would not allow them to enter into this paradise. Most firmly I kept at bay thoughts of the occupants in the house at the top of the hill across the river. Yet I could not keep out fear. But it was a sweet fear. . . . I didn't want him to kiss me again for a little while, so I began to talk.

All kinds of things were happening to me for the first time tonight. I had Ronnie's urge to talk, and strangely enough I found myself talking about him. But not so strangely, for there was a desire in me to impress Martin in some other way than with my looks, and to talk of our Ronnie was the only way I could do it, for there was no topic I could discuss except cooking and housework for I couldn't talk about the wood or the river. These were my feelings and I had not the power of words with which to translate them.

But what did my talking result in? Only a slight feeling of pique when I realized Martin was amused by what I was saying. And when he said, 'And what books does Ronnie read?' I couldn't think of one title. Then to my aid came the incident of the day when he had answered the priest, and I said, with an assumed casualness, 'Oh, well, books like "Martin Luther".'

Instantly, I saw that he was impressed, and for the first time his tone held a note that was not nice, there was something, was it condescension as he said, 'Well, well, so we've got traitors among us. Your brother is a boy after my own heart.'

'Father Ellis didn't think so,' I laughed.

'You're a Catholic, Christine?'

I nodded.

'And your brother reads Martin Luther? I can see why the priest didn't like it.' He seemed amused.

'Are you a Catholic?' I asked shyly.

His head went back and he laughed, 'Good Lord, no!' Then he said softly, 'Oh, I'm sorry, Christine, I didn't mean it like that. I'm nothing. I'm searching, like your brother's doing. He must be if he's reading Luther.'

His mood changed and he exclaimed, 'Luther! A summer night like this, the most beautiful girl in the world – and you are you know – a flowing river, and here we are talking about Luther.... Let me look at you.' He pulled me round to face him. 'I want to look at your face, all the time, forever. You're like a star on a dung heap.'

As his eyes washed my face and his fingers outlined the curve of my mouth, I felt I was going to sink into the glory of oblivion – or was it of living – yet at the same time a pocket in my mind, the pocket that was holding thoughts of my mother and Dad and our Ronnie, was now urging me to get up and get my dress and go home. So much did my thoughts clamour that they burst their confines and I heard myself whisper, 'Will you see if my dress is dry?'

He gave a deep, soft laugh, then said, 'All right,' and springing up he went to the bushes. I saw him lift my dress in his hands, and then he called, 'It's slightly damp on the other side, I'll turn it over.' In a second he was at my side again. 'Look at me,' he said, and when I did so he added, 'I don't want to take my eyes off you.'

There followed a pause, during which I became filled with awe. That I, Christine Winter, could find such favour in the eyes of this god, this god from another planet.

'It's going to be a long, beautiful summer, Christine.'

I, too felt it was going to be a long, beautiful summer, and when his arms went about me I made no protest, but just leant against him. I had no urge now as I had a little while ago to ask questions: where did he live when he wasn't visiting on Brampton Hill, or at Oxford? Or where he was going when he left Brampton Hill? Or whether now he had found me he would stay on Brampton Hill? I had no desire to have an answer to any of these questions, for he had said, 'It's going to be a long, beautiful summer.'

The twilight was deepening, and soon it would be dusk and I must be home before dark, and I hated the thought of leaving this spot, of ever moving out of the circle of his arms. It did not seem the slightest bit out of place that he was wearing only bathing trunks, for I was used to the sight of our Ronnie and Don and Sam in bathing trunks. What I wasn't used to was the sight of my own bare legs against theirs, yet now, as I looked down towards my feet, I felt not the slightest embarrassment, only an intense joy at the contact of Martin's instep across my foot.

Then I could no longer look down at my feet, for he had turned my face towards him again and was holding me close, and there descended on my mind and body and all the world a stillness, and within the stillness I lay awake. What followed was inevitable, nothing could have stopped it, for I had no strength within myself to combat such a force, my religion and upbringing were as useless as if they had never existed. I was sent soaring into the heavens, higher than any bird, and when I floated down to earth again I was crying. Unrestrainedly and helplessly, I was crying. My arms, bare now, were about his neck, and I sobbed out this bewilderment of feeling. Then as quickly as my crying had begun it stopped, and I wanted to laugh. I made a small sound like a laugh, and it broke on a hiccup, and in a moment we were both laughing into each other's necks. I wanted to laugh louder and louder. I felt bodyless, there was nothing left of me but laughter. And this told me I was gloriously, ecstatically, blissfully happy. I was drunk with the wine of creation, oblivious for the moment to everything but bliss. And then the heavens opened and God spoke.

'CHRISTINE!'

My name thundered over me, and went rolling along the

river, and instinctively I broke away from Martin's arms and buried my face in the earth.

'CHRISTINE, GET UP!'

I shuddered and trembled and raised myself a little way on my hands, and from under my lids I saw Martin's feet turn swiftly towards the edge of the bank, then drop to the beach where his clothes were.

I put one hand and groped wildly for the coat, but could feel nothing. Then my dress descended on me, and Father Ellis's voice cried, 'Cover yourself, girl! Before God, I cannot believe it's you!'

In a mad frenzy of fear now, I pulled the dress over my head, but I still remained kneeling on the ground, terrified to get to my feet. Father Ellis's black-clothed legs were before me, the high polish on his black boots seemed to pierce the dusk. Then they turned from me and moved towards the edge of the bank, and his voice, rasping out in command, cried, 'Come here, you!'

Ironically now I was praying. Oh, Blessed Virgin Mary, don't let him say anything to Martin. Please! Please! don't let him. Then his voice cut through my agonized praying mind, yelling, 'Come here! Come here, I say.'

I raised my eyes and saw Father Ellis jumping down the bank. Then on the dull sound of pounding feet I staggered up and, going to the edge, I saw something that stripped the night of wonder and brought my god low, for Martin was running along the bank in great leaping strides and, almost as swiftly, Father Ellis was after him. But I was praying again, 'Don't let him catch him! don't let him catch him!' for I couldn't bear that Martin should suffer the indignity of being dragged back here by Father Ellis, not that he would allow himself to be dragged anywhere. I had a terrifying picture of him striking out at the priest.

Lowering myself quickly down the bank, I got into my shoes and stockings, and when I again stood up it was to see Father Ellis coming towards me – alone.

I have not the power of words with which to describe the mixture of feelings that were raging through me as I stood with my head bowed waiting for the priest's approach. I only knew that they centred around a great humiliation, and I wanted to die, to drop down dead on the spot.

I was looking down once more on to the shiny black boots, but they were some distance from me, and the distance the priest had left between us spoke to me of my degradation in his eyes more plainly than his words had done. The seconds ticked by and he did not speak, and I found myself swaying as if I was going to faint. And when he muttered in a strange voice, 'I just can't believe it. You . . . you, Christine. . . . How long has this been going on? Answer me!' The last words were said in a tone he had never used to me before, more like a bark, and I muttered, 'Just tonight, Father.'

'How long have you known him?'

How long had I known him? All my life, from the minute I started breathing he had been there. This wonderful, pale-faced, beautiful-voiced god. But could I answer now, 'Two nights,' or 'a week,' or 'since just after Easter'?

'Answer me.'

'Just . . . just a short time, Father.'

'How short?'

I couldn't bring myself to say 'Two nights', for it now seemed an impossibility that there had been so much love crammed into two nights, so I muttered, 'A week.'

'God! God!' The priest's exclamation sounded like deep swearing, and my shoulders sank down, dragging my head with them.

'What's his name?'

I paused, trying to gain the strength to refuse to answer, but it was useless. 'Martin Fonyère, Father.'

'Where does he live?'

'On . . . on Brampton Hill.'

'There are lots of people living on Brampton Hill, I want his address.'

My body seemed almost bent in two, so deep was my shame.

'Do you hear, Christine?'

'I – I don't know, Father.'

He did not speak again for some minutes, but I could hear his breathing, quick and hissing in the quiet around us. Then he said abruptly, 'Come along home.'

My body jerked up straight, and my eyes seemed to jump from my head to his grey face, and I repeated, 'Home, Father?' Then I gabbled, 'You won't tell me mam?'

'She must be told. Have you thought of the consequences of this night's escapade?'

'But, Father—' I had stepped towards him – 'you can't tell me mam, she's bad ... ill, you know she is, and she doesn't know anything about ...'

'All the more reason why she must be told.' His voice was cold now, dead sounding, without feeling.

'No, Father, no! ... Please! please! Oh, don't tell me mam, please!' In desperation, I flung myself on the ground at his feet and grabbed hold of his trouser leg, and as I touched it, I felt his flesh recoiling from my hand as if it had been stung, and his voice was loud and angry once more as he cried, 'Get up!'

'No, Father, no! I won't move from here, I won't! You can't tell her. I'll drown meself, I will! I will! You can't tell her!'

'Leave go!' He put down his hand to remove my fingers, but before it touched me, he quickly drew it away again, and with a tug from his leg he freed himself. Then again standing some distance from me, he said, 'All right, I promise I won't tell her, but on one condition.'

I raised my tear-misted eyes to his now unfamiliar face, and then he said, 'You will never see that man again.'

My stomach retched, my heart seemed to turn over. Never to see Martin again, never to hear his voice. I couldn't, I couldn't promise, not at this moment I couldn't. A little earlier as I had watched him fleeing before the priest, in that brief moment perhaps I could have promised, but I couldn't now, and I said, 'I can't, Father, I can't.'

'Very well then, come home.'

When I got to my feet, my body seemed dragged down, as if I was carrying a bucket of coal in each hand, and my legs would not obey me and walk. I felt myself swaying and I muttered, 'I – I feel faint, Father.' As I felt myself falling, I sunk down to the ground but willed myself not to faint, and in a few minutes I got to my feet again.

I kept my eyes turned from the priest and made to walk on when his voice stopped me.

'Go home,' he said, 'I won't tell your mother anything yet. I don't believe you don't know where this man lives, but I'll find him quite easily, I have ways and means, and he must marry you right away.'

At this I turned wide, startled eyes on to his face, but found I couldn't say anything, not a word, for to my amazement I saw through the fading light that Father Ellis was crying, and at the sight a sorrow pierced me very like the day I had seen the rabbit nailed to the tree. Flinging myself about I ran stumbling and sobbing along the bank, and when I crossed the stones it was to meet our Ronnie. He pulled me to a stop and stared at me before exclaiming angrily, 'Where d'you think you've been to at this time of night? Mam's worried stiff.' Then looking me up and down he added, 'Good Lord! what's happened to you?'

My sorrow broke loose and burying my face in my hands, I cried and spluttered, 'I – I fell in the river – and – waited until – until my clothes dried.'

'Aw, never mind.' His voice was soft, softer than it had been for a long time. 'Come on,' he said. The instant I felt his arms going round me, I tore myself away from him like a mad thing, and, running as if my very life depended on it, I made for home.

CHAPTER FOUR

My mother said, 'You're ill, girl, you must see the doctor. That tumble into the river frightened you, and this is the after-effects. You look like a ghost.'

'I'm all right,' I said.

'But you're not, lass. You look like death, and you're not yourself in any way, and you're not going to go walking by that river by yourself at night again.'

'Oh, Mam!' I exclaimed hurriedly, 'I like walking by the river.'

'Well, then, you'll let Ronnie go with you.'

'No!' The tone even startled myself, and, coming to me, she looked into my face and said, 'What is it, lass? I've never known you to be like this. You're not frightened of all this war talk, are you?'

War talk. What did the war talk matter to me, with my own war raging inside me?

'War talk?' I said. 'No, of course not.'

I mustn't have sounded very convincing, for she added, comfortingly, 'There won't be any gas in this war, that's if it comes, and God knows it looks very much like it. They saw what gas did in the last one. They've learnt something, they won't act like mad animals again. Although that Hitler seems like a maniac.'

War, war, digging trenches and air-raid shelters and getting fitted for gasmasks, in their silly little boxes, and people storing in food, buying up everything they could, and men in different trades being stood off because they couldn't get the material with which to carry on their jobs. Everybody waiting for the war to start. Our Ronnie saying he was going to join up and looking at me as he said it. Don Dowling saying they wouldn't get him. Anyway, pitmen were exempt if they worked at the coal face. Then yesterday my mother sending me with her wedding-ring down to the pawnshop in Bog's End to get a little extra money to buy tin stuff to store away . . . just in case, as she said. Then going to Woolworths and buying her a ring there. This all unknown to Dad, for she said he wouldn't have stood for it. Her little duplicity pleased her, I saw, yet I could take no part in it. I could take no part in anything that went on in the house or outside, for I was dead.

I had gone down to the river bank on the Sunday night and walked and walked its length between the stepping stones and the big bend several times, but he hadn't come. There had been another couple lying in the green hollow, surrounded by the bushes, and our Ronnie had come looking for me again and demanded roughly, 'What you doing prowling the bank? You after a lad?'

He had gripped my arm and I had wrenched it angrily away from him, crying, 'And if I was it's none of your business!' And he, like Father Ellis, had looked amazed for a moment, before saying, 'Well, I thought you could have got one without going on the prowl.' As I have said the river bank was given over to the courting couples on a Sunday night and to groups of lads and lasses out for the sole purpose of clicking. But as we neared the house his tone had become solicitous and he inquired softly, 'What is it, Christine? There is something up with you. Can't you talk to me about it?' It was the only time during the past week that I was tempted to laugh.

Every night I went to the river, and if I had to go into the town during the day I made my way round to the better-class shopping centre at the foot of Brampton Hill, my eyes searching all the while.

The following Saturday night I stood in a warm drizzling rain looking up at the gardens on the hill across from the big bend and praying, 'Oh, Martin, Martin, please come. I'll die if I don't see you. I will, I will. Oh, Martin, Martin! Please God make him come. Oh, Holy Mother, answer my prayer.' Yet as I prayed I knew he wouldn't come. But even with this knowledge deep inside me, I kept asking, 'Why? Why?' He surely must come if only because of the fact that I needed him and wanted to see him, to hear him, to be pressed close to him and feel his eyes moving over my face, feel his look burying itself in me. And then there was this frightening urge of my body that I had to fight each night. . . . Oh, Martin! Martin!

As I turned homewards I saw through the drizzle a figure coming along the river bank, but there was no leaping of my heart and I didn't think, 'That's Martin', I knew who it was. The black felt hat, the black mackintosh, the black trousers and the black boots. When Father Ellis stood in front of me I did not lower my head this time, I kept it level, but I turned my gaze away and looked over the river.

'Well, Christine?' His voice was one that I recognized. There was the old kindliness in it. I did not say, 'Hallo, Father,' I made no remark whatever, yet I was glad to see him and I longed for him to speak, for when he did he would give me some news of Martin. Perhaps he would say he had refused to marry me. And would it be any wonder? All beauty, all magic stripped from our lives by a compulsory order to marry.

I walked on and the priest turned and walked by my side. We had gone a considerable distance before he spoke, and then it seemed it was with an effort that he asked, 'Have you seen that man again, Christine?'

'No, Father.'

'Were you speaking the truth when you said you didn't know where he lived?'

'Yes, Father.'

'I made a boast last Saturday night that I'd find him. Well, I haven't been able to. Apparently there is no one of that name living on Brampton Hill, or even visiting there.'

The leaping of my heart, the turning of my stomach, brought me round and I gazed on him and protested, 'But he does live there, in one of the houses that have the gardens backing on to the river.'

'You mean Fell Close or The Rise, and round about there? I have access into most of those houses, he doesn't live there. What is more I would recognize him again in a moment.' He was standing looking down on me now, compassion in his face, and he asked, 'Oh, what have you done, Christine? Let's hope God is merciful to you.'

I pressed my hand over my mouth and cried, 'Oh, don't start on me, Father, not again.'

'All right, all right. But I want you to promise me something, Christine.'

I stumbled on, taking no heed until he said, 'I want you to promise to come to mass every morning for the next three months.'

My eyes looked vacantly ahead as I muttered, 'I can't get every morning, Father; there's too much to see to in the house.'

'Well, when you can.'

He crossed the stones with me, and as we reached the bottom of the river bank, below our houses, Ronnie came down the hill and Sam with him. Before they reached us the priest had left me without even a word of good-bye. But he waved his hand to them and they waved back.

When they came up to me, Ronnie remarked, 'He's in a hurry the night.' Then taking my arm, he said, 'You come on up home and get to bed, you look as if you are in for something. You're mad, out in this drizzle.'

I said nothing but let him lead me up the hill. Sam, on my other side, said, 'I've made you another plaque with your surname on it, Christine,' and before we reached our door and I fainted, I remember thinking, 'Kind Sam, nice Sam.'

'But I assure you, Mrs. Winter, she is pregnant.'

'But . . . but, doctor, she can't be!'

'I understand it must be very difficult for you to take it in, but I assure you that that is her condition.'

I stood in the little room off the surgery getting into my clothes. My hands were shaking so that I couldn't fasten them up. Then for almost the sixth time since the doctor had joined my mother, I heard her explain, in high amazement, 'But, doctor!' Then, her voice in a terrible whisper, she exclaimed, 'But how can she, she never goes out with anyone, she's never been with anyone?'

The buttons were slipping away from my fingers as if possessed of a life of their own, and there was a pause before the doctor spoke again. 'She has had intercourse, Mrs. Winter.'

Every organ in my body was shaking with terror, and as automatically I smoothed the front of my dress over my stomach, my fingers drew sharply away from contact with it. Inside there was something vile and awful, a thing that was bringing horror into my mother's voice. I pushed myself towards the door, and when I entered the surgery, my mother stared at me as if she had never seen me before, and I noticed her reactions were similar to those of Father Ellis. She kept her distance, she even stepped back from me. When the doctor opened the door and we had passed out she still did not come near me, and we walked all the way home separated by an arm's length. And she uttered not a word until she got into the kitchen. Then sitting down in a chair by the table, she dropped her head on to her hands and burst into passionate weeping. Helplessly, I stood watching her, the tears raining down my face. And as I stood like this the back door opened and my dad came in from the allotment, accompanied by Ronnie, who was on back shift. The sound of their entry aroused me from my stupor, and I made to go upstairs when my mother, without looking at me, put out her hand and said, 'You stay here.'

Immediately on entering the kitchen Dad exclaimed, 'What's up?' Then going to my mother he asked anxiously, 'What is it, Annie? What's happened?' He looked from one to the other, and my mother, drawing herself up by the aid of the table, said, 'You'd better know sooner or later. There's a reason for her sickness these weeks, she's going to have a bairn.'

'Bairn?' The look on Dad's face could have been comic. His lips were drawn back from his teeth and his eyes were lost behind the pushed up flesh on his cheeks. But Ronnie's look was not comic. The colour had fled from his fresh-coloured face and his eyes looked terrible, fearsome and full of loathing, and he yelled right out loud as if he was on the open hillside, 'No! God, no!' Dad came slowly to me and, taking my hand gently, said, 'Look at me, lass.'

And when I could not look at him he dropped my hand exclaiming, 'Christ Almighty!' And my mother repeated, 'Aye, Christ Almighty.' Then Dad, turning to me again, said sternly, 'Who's the fella?' But before waiting for my answer he swung round to my mother, crying as if I wasn't there, 'But I've never known her to go out with a lad.'

'No,' said my mother, in dead sounding tones, 'she's had

no need. You haven't far to seek. It's been coming for years. I've seen it coming for years and dreaded this moment.'

These words brought my head up and a wave of protest through my body and I cried, 'It wasn't him, not Don Dowling.'

'What!' My mother was staring at me. 'Then who was it?' The deadness had left her voice and now she looked angry, threateningly angry, as she demanded, 'Who was it? Where have you been?'

I cast my eyes towards our Ronnie, and Dad turned to him and said, 'Go on out.'

Ronnie went out, but he backed from the room and his eyes never left my face until he had passed through the door and into the scullery.

Dad now going to the scullery door pulled it shut, then he joined my mother and, side by side, they stood looking at me.

With my hands gripped tightly together and my eyes fixed on the floor, I said, 'It was a boy I got to know.' I did not wait for them to ask his name but continued, 'They called him Martin Fonyère, he lives on Brampton Hill.' I still did not believe what the priest had said that Martin did not live on the Hill.

'Then we must have a talk with him.'

I raised my eyes when Dad spoke, and what I saw on his face was too much for me, for there, untouched, was his love still shining but threaded now with pity and compassion. I turned slowly about and leaning against the wall I buried my face in the crook of my arm and sobbed helplessly. . . .

It was a week later and Martin Fonyère had become someone who had never existed, at least to my mother and Dad. My mother was becoming frantic to find him and make him marry me before the scandal became obvious, and at this moment she had just returned from Mrs. Durrant's. Mrs. Durrant had lived on the Hill for years and she knew nearly everybody of any importance there. My mother had confided the whole business to her and she had suggested that the most likely place to find this elusive fellow was The Grange, for a number of young men were staying there, and not to ask for an appointment but to take me and go boldly up there and ask for Colonel Findlay.

I cried and protested but I could do nothing to deter her, and so, standing in a flame of shame, I found myself on the wide steps of The Grange listening to my mother asking to speak to this Colonel Findlay.

The colonel was tall and thin and never stopped moving about as my mother spoke, and although he scared me with his blustering my mother remained unperturbed, answering him calmly, saying, 'I'm not accusing anyone, I'm just asking you if you have anyone staying here by the name of Martin Fonyère and could we please speak to him?'

'There's no Martin Fonyère here,' said the colonel. 'I have two nephews staying in the house at present and my two sons. There they are on the tennis court. Here.' He lifted a sharp finger and beckoned me to the window. 'Is the young man you are seeking among those?'

I looked out of the great window on to the tennis court and the four men jumping about. Not one of them was anything like Martin and I shook my head slowly, and without waiting I walked towards the door. The colonel was speaking again to my mother asking her who had told her to come here.

As I stood just within the door waiting for her I found myself looking at a picture on a side table. It showed a group of children, three boys and two girls; they were about fourteen years of age and were all sitting in a row on a balustrade and the second one from the end was Martin Fonyère. As clearly as one would recognize oneself in a mirror I knew it was he. The long, pale face, the brown hair, that penetrating, dark, intense look already in his eyes. It was Martin, and this was the house where he had stayed. What relation he was to the people here I did not know, but what I did know was that the Colonel had been aware of us even before he had seen us, and in a flash of insight I knew I had Father Ellis to thank for this. His diplomatic investigations had been broadcast to this house as a warning against coming trouble ... Catholic priest trouble. Priests had the power to bring about unusual things, even the power to force a man from Brampton Hill to marry a girl from Fenwick Houses, or at least ensure her of support.

My mother's steps were behind me and I moved forward into the hall, and if I wanted any further proof that this was the house where Martin had lived I had it as I came face to

face with a young woman. She was much older than me, perhaps twenty-two or three. She stared at me as if wanting to
remember my face forever, and as I looked back at her I
thought, 'You were likely his girl before he met me, and hope
to be again.'

'Eileen!'

It was a sharp voice calling from the stairway and the girl
slowly drew her eyes from me and walked away. Then the
colonel opened the door and let us out, and my mother said,
'Thank you.' But he said nothing.

War was declared but it made no impact on our house, I
had already dropped the bomb that had blown our peace to
smithereens. My mother seemed to have thrown off her
illness and become possessed of an energy that enabled her to
search and inquire. And I did nothing to stop her, for I was
numb inside and not caring what happened to myself or to
anyone else. This feeling was dominant in me until the night
our Ronnie spoke.

My mother had come in from one of her visits to Mrs.
Durrant. I was upstairs at the time, but my door was open and
I heard her remark, 'The earth couldn't have opened and
swallowed him up, he must be somewhere. If he was in the
town somebody must have remembered him.' And then I
heard our Ronnie say, 'Perhaps he never was.'

'What do you mean?' said my mother.

'It's only somebody she's made up.'

'Oh, lad, I wish it was, how I wish to God it was. But she
couldn't, she hasn't made up the bairn. And if it isn't Don,
and she says it isn't, who could it be?'

'Have you ever thought of Father Ellis?'

My hands went to my mouth and almost stopped my
breathing, then I was on the landing, down the stairs and in
the kitchen before my mother had repeated for the second
time an agonized 'No!' It was a high 'No!' like a wail, and as
her voice drifted away I almost sprang on our Ronnie, crying,
'You! you devil you.' Then turning to Mam, I screamed,
'You can't believe him. It was Martin Fonyère. There is a
Martin Fonyère.'

Our Ronnie's eyes were like slits and he was apparently
unperturbed by my onslaught, but his voice was bitter as he

brought out, 'What about the night I met you on the river bank with him, and he scuttled away? Shortly after that you were in this state, you passed out. Explain that.'

'You! you wicked devil. What if I tell Mam? What if I tell Mam?' I was spluttering in my rage, and as I spluttered a voice warned me to be quiet, warned me that my mother had enough on her plate without telling her this thing about our Ronnie that would surely drive her mad.

I swung round to her, crying, 'Mam, believe me, for God's sake believe me, there is a Martin Fonyère.'

'Well, it's a funny thing, lass, nobody has seen him but you.' My mother's voice was quiet and tired now, and at this moment I remembered Sam. 'Wait!' I cried. 'Wait a minute.' I dashed out through the scullery, down our backyard, into the backlane, up Aunt Phyllis's backyard and, bursting open her door, cried, 'Where's Sam, Aunt Phyllis?'

She was sitting at the table with Don, and they both rose to their feet together.

'What's up?' asked Don. I shook my head, still looking at Aunt Phyllis, and demanded, 'Where's Sam?'

'Upstairs.'

'Get him.' I had never spoken to her in this fashion in my life, but she seemed not to notice and called, 'Sam! You, Sam, come down here.'

Within a minute Sam was in the kitchen, and to his astonishment, and certainly to the bewilderment of Aunt Phyllis and even of Don, I grabbed his hand and ran him through the two backyards and into our kitchen.

Thrusting the bewildered boy in front of my mother, I almost glared at him as I said, 'Sam, tell Mam what I asked you to promise not to tell anybody.'

He turned startled eyes upon me and said below his breath, 'About – about the lad, Christine?' I nodded quickly.

Sam looked at my mother and said very slowly, 'I promised Christine not to let on that she was out with a lad, Aunt Annie.'

As if a great load had been lifted from my mother's back she sat down in her chair and pulled Sam towards her.

'You saw Christine with a lad, Sam?'

'Yes, Aunt Annie.'

'Can you tell me what he looked like?'

Sam glanced back at me and I said, 'Tell her, tell her everything, Sam.'

'Well,' Sam said, 'he was tallish like, Aunt Annie.'

'As tall as Ronnie?'

'No, taller, like our Don. But thin, he was very thin and he had brown hair.'

'Is there anything else you remember?'

'He wore nice clothes, Aunt Annie.'

'Where did you see him with Christine?'

'They were walking along the river bank.'

'When?'

'Oh, one night a few weeks ago, that time it was very hot.'

'Thanks, Sam,' said my mother, and when Sam turned from her I put out my hand and touched his shoulder. I was unable to speak but my eyes spoke my thanks. Then I turned on Ronnie and, looking him full in the face, I said, 'I'll never forgive you for this, not as long as I live.' I went upstairs again and threw myself on the bed and cried and sobbed until I couldn't breathe, and felt that I would choke to death. Then the door opened and my mother's arm came round me for the first time in weeks, and I turned and clung to her, crying, 'Oh! Mam, Mam, I'm sorry.'

As she patted my head she kept saying, 'There now, there now. Tell me all about it, how it happened.'

It was odd that she had never asked that in the first place. And so, sitting side by side on the bed, I told her everything, or nearly so, and we were near again. Then she said, 'Come on downstairs and we'll have a cup of tea.' And she pulled me up from the bed. But as we got to the door she stopped and, jerking her head towards the bedroom wall, she looked at me and stated, 'They've got to know sooner or later.'

My mother made it sooner, likely thinking to get it over and done with. It was the next afternoon that she told Aunt Phyllis. I did not know she was going to tell her then, and I was at the table rolling out some pastry when I heard the commotion. It was coming from Aunt Phyllis's yard, but the next minute when I glanced towards the window I saw Don come tearing up our yard, my mother after him, her hand outstretched as if trying to catch hold of him.

When he appeared at the kitchen door I was standing ready waiting, for in this moment I had no fear of him. Strangely,

I felt strong and fortified against him. The sight of me standing thus halted him, and my mother pressed by him and stood in between us. And her voice was loud as she cried, 'Now, Don Dowling, this is nothing to do with you.'

'No, begod! no. No, it isn't.' He turned on her with a terrible smile. 'No, you saw to that, you padded her all over, her bloody breasts and everything, in case anybody looked at her. You're to blame for this if the truth were told. You wouldn't let me have her. Oh, no. Oh, I knew what you thought, I wasn't good enough, and now some bugger has given her a bellyful and skedaddled. And in a way I could laugh, laugh like hell at you. . . .'

On my mother's cry of 'Get out!' he turned his face from her but did not move, and he looked at me. His eyes were hooded with a dark light, and from it I could feel pouring malevolence so powerful that I seemed to smell it, it was like a stench. And when I thought of this later I told myself it was my imagination and my inborn fear of him that had created this illusion, for whereas I had felt no fear of him while waiting for him to enter the kitchen, from the moment he spoke I began to tremble, so that my mother intervened again, crying, 'If you don't get out this minute I'll let you have this.' She swung round and grabbed the poker and advanced threateningly on him. One thrust from his great hand and she would have been on her back. But he did not lift his hand, he simply let his gaze linger on me for a moment longer, then said on a grating laugh, 'The town will be full of soldiers in a week or two, I'll tell them where they can be supplied.'

'You! . . . You! Get out!' My mother actually brought the poker down on him, but he side-stepped and thrust her aside as if she were the weight of a child. Then, turning on his heel, he went out.

Slowly my mother moved to the fireplace and put the poker back into the hearth. I sat down by the table and rested my head on the palm of my hand, and she came and stood beside me and in a trembling voice she said a comforting thing. 'Don't shake so, lass,' she said; 'he can do nothing to you now. You have taken it out of his power, and for that I could even say "thank God", for I'd rather see you in the pickle you're in than married to him.'

The reactions to my condition were many and varied, and we had more visitors to the house in the next few weeks than we'd had in years, on one pretext or another. But it was my Aunt Phyllis's reactions that amazed me most. She was civil to me, even kind. And I worked it out that this attitude was due to her being relieved of her jealousy. No longer was I acceptable to Don; there was no danger now that at any moment I would take her son from her. But later I think she even wished he had got me, for he was creating a name for himself among the women in Bog's End that outdid that of the soldiers. He and I did not meet for some weeks, and so I did not know whether or not he would have spoken to me, even in abuse. But Ronnie and I met every day – it was impossible sometimes not to rub shoulders – yet he never opened his mouth to me. Mam was kind and understanding, and as the days went on I became thankful for her sake that the war was on, for people were more concerned with the day-to-day news of it than they were in the shame I had brought on her. Only Dad remained the same. Yet not the same, he was more loving and considerate of me than ever before. As for Sam, he followed me around, saying little but always there, his kind eyes telling me that to him I was still Christine, the old Christine.

And what about myself? I laughed no longer, I could not even smile. At night, up in my room in the candlelight, I looked at my swelling body and had not even the strength to hate it. Quicker than I had fallen into the river I had fallen into life and I was stunned by it. I could not even find the heart in me to condemn the perpetrator, although I knew that Martin had not only run away from the priest, but had scuttled away from the house on the hill, aided, no doubt, by the colonel. In spite of all this I longed to see him, and the longing was at its height when I lay down in bed at night. For hours my eyes would stare through the window at the dark sky and my heart would be talking to him, pleading with him to come back. There was no call to him from my body now, that was taken up with the thing inside me. I did not think of it as a baby, but as something I would have to suffer and carry for the rest of my life because I had sinned, and grievously. I did not have to see the look in Father Ellis's eyes, on his odd visits, to know this. The terrifying thing was I knew with an absolute certainty that if Martin were to come back and the occasion to sin presented itself to me again I should be powerless to make any resistance. And this knowledge revealed to me more than anything else how weak I was where I loved, how weak I was altogether for I could not even hate properly – Martin, our Ronnie, or anyone else – at least not yet.

The war had been on six months, people had stopped sleeping in the air-raid shelters every night, and the song of the moment was 'We're Going to Hang Out the Washing on the Siegfried Line'. One morning early, about four o'clock, Dad came up to my room and woke me saying he would have to go for the doctor for Mam. By nine o'clock that morning my mother was in hospital. Three days later she died saying, 'Christine, my Christine. Oh, lass, oh, lass.' And the world went on with its business of fighting, but our house became a thing apart, like a deserted planet. The rooms seemed much larger and completely empty, and Dad turned into an old man within a week, and instead of he being my prop I now became his. I could not believe my mother had gone, and I cried unceasingly for days, but Dad did not cry. He seemed to be dried out, and the fact that I became worried about him took my mind somewhat from myself and also made me forget, at least for intervals, the fear of the coming event, the fear of giving birth to the baby, the fear of the pain that would rend me in two, as Aunt Phyllis had described it to me.

Dad was working again, and he and Ronnie were on the same shift. For hours at a stretch I would have the house to myself, and I would be so lonely at times that I wished I was with my mother. I never left the house unless I had to, and then I tried to arrange it when Ronnie would be indoors, thus giving me less time to suffer his silent condemnation. And though I was thankful that people now had less time to be concerned with the scandals around them, when Mrs. Campbell became a regular visitor to my Aunt Phyllis's kitchen, as also did Miss Spiers from the end house, I did not have to think deeply to imagine the gist of their conversation.

I was getting so big now that I did not want to be seen. I had no pride within me to keep my head defiantly high, and my laugh that could have sustained me, or at least formed a façade about my true feelings, was dead within me. So, with no attempt to titivate myself up, I would go down into town to get the groceries. And on one such visit I ran into Mollie. She must have been aware of what had befallen me for otherwise she would have made some comment on my rotund figure, but she seemed very pleased to see me, even delighted, and wanted me to go and have a cup of tea with her. She told me she was working in the munitions factory, and ended, 'What do you think? I've got a place of me own, two rooms and a kitchen By! I wouldn't call the Queen me aunt.' Then she had grabbed hold of my hand and said, 'Come and see me, Christine, will you? It's 21B Gordon Street.' And I smiled at her and promised I would. She must have felt a bit awkward with me for she had not sworn once.

Christmas came and added to the nightmare of my existence, for at this time I seemed to miss my mother more than I had done immediately after she died. As for Dad, his sorrow and loneliness were such that I wanted to cry every time I looked at him. How Ronnie was affected I did not know, for he showed the same taciturn face which had become usual with him.

By the end of March my body was so distorted that I became sick with the sight of it. Only when you have a husband and are carrying something for him can your bloated and stretched skin take on the appearance of beauty, but when there is no one to call this thing 'ours' and it remains yours alone, it is impossible to see beauty in it.

At seven o'clock on a Friday night towards the end of March, as the air-raid siren screeched a warning over the town, a fiery pain brought my swollen limbs to a sudden halt. I was at the cupboard getting my coat before going over to the shelter, and I found myself transfixed, one foot forward, one hand outstretched, my mouth open and my breath seemingly stopped. When I managed to reach a chair I thought, this is it. I was alone in the house and I became terrified – Aunt Phyllis would be already in the shelter. But just then I heard footsteps hurrying up the backyard. It would be Dad. I kept my eyes on the door but it was Ronnie who came through it. He stared at me for a moment and I tried to speak, to tell him to go for Aunt Phyllis, but I could not for the pain had come again. Then he had hold of my hand and he was talking, but gently: 'Come on, lie down. Oh, my God! To see you in a state like this. Oh! Christine.'

I realized that he was crying and some part of me outside of the pain was horrified at this and was yelling, 'No! no! I don't want him to be sorry,' for if he were sorry for me all the old business would start again. I remember pushing him aside and getting up and saying between gasps, 'Go and get Aunt Phyllis,' and of being surprised when, immediately, like an obedient child, he ran out of the kitchen and through the front door, which was the nearest way to the shelter, to bring her.

Eighteen hours later the child was born, and Aunt Phyllis had been right about the pain. It was a girl with a face the shape of Martin's, and I had no interest in it.

The next night Don Dowling came in roaring drunk and sang and shouted in their front room, and since I was lying in Dad's bed in our front room it was as if he was standing by my side. When Aunt Phyllis came in to see me she made no comment whatever about the oration, and the situation should have appeared weird but I was so weak and dazed that her strange attitude must have seemed simply part of the pattern of this awful, pain-filled thing called living. But when the nurse came in for the night visit she hammered on the wall, shouting, 'If you don't cease that noise I'll go and get a policeman.'

Aunt Phyllis was in our kitchen when this occurred, and shortly afterwards she went in next door and there was no more noise. Vaguely it occurred to me that she could have stopped it sooner.

It was the first of June, nineteen-forty, a beautiful day, warm and mellow, and the wireless was telling of the evacuation from Dunkirk. There had been no 'washing hanging on the Seigfried Line' after all. I was standing in the scullery doing the dinner dishes. Outside in the yard, in her pram, lay Constance. Why I had called the child Constance I don't really know, maybe because it expressed my feelings for her father, constant, ever constant, and alongside this love there was growing daily for this child I had not wanted another kind of love. Now, when I took her in my arms and fed her, I knew I was no longer whole, part of me was in her.

She had also brought a feeling of family back into the house; she had, I knew, eased my father's pain, and his love for her was as deep as, if not deeper than, the love he had for me.

Ronnie paid little attention to her – he would glance at her but never spoke to her or talked the baby twaddle that Dad did and which, strangely, I found it impossible to use – but to my growing concern he had once again turned his attention to me. He was all forgiveness and solicitude, and this solicitude did more to bring me back into an awareness of life than anything else, because it created in me the old fear. I was now sleeping upstairs again, and each night I dreaded a midnight visit . . . just to talk.

As I finished the dishes Sam came up the yard and stood by the pram, looking down on the child and touching her with his finger, and he turned and smiled at me through the scullery window. Then coming in, he said, 'By, she's bonnie, Christine.'

I smiled at him, there was no need for words with Sam.

'Where's Stinker?' he asked. 'I'll take him for a run on the fells.'

'I haven't seen him since the middle of the morning, Sam,' I replied; 'he should be in for his dinner, he's never this late.'

I was never to see Stinker again. He did not come in all day, and Dad, as he had done once before, searched the fells for him. On the Sunday, remembering where Don had found him in the stables, Dad visited them again, but there was no sign of a dog of any kind, nor had anyone noticed the children playing with a strange dog.

When he brought this news back I began to cry. 'Now, now, lass,' he said, 'you know what dogs are, he's gone on the rampage. In about three days he'll show up, tired and hungry. It's the nature of the beast.'

Three days passed and Stinker did not show up, and on Tuesday afternoon a man came to ask if he could see Dad. I told him he was down on the allotment. An hour later Dad came slowly into the scullery, the blue marks on his forehead where the coal had left its design were standing out visibly. He came straight to the point, patting my shoulder and saying, 'Prepare yourself for a bit of a shock, lass. . . . Stinker's dead.'

'Oh, Dad, no!' I sank down on to a chair and said in a whisper, 'Where?' and then, 'How?'

I watched him draw the back of his hand across both sides of his mouth before replying, 'He was drowned, lass.'

I was on my feet now. 'He couldn't drown, Dad, he was a swimmer, he couldn't drown.'

Dad filled his chest with air and let it out slowly before speaking again. 'He was drowned, lass, in a sack filled with bricks.'

I closed my eyes, then pressed my palms over them, but it didn't shut out the picture of Stinker in the sack full of bricks. Dad's voice was going on, rising in anger, but I only heard snatches of what he was saying, such as 'I'll make the swine pay for this. I'll find out before I die who did the day's work, by God! I will.'

Oh! Stinker. Poor Stinker, with his shaggy coat and his warm tongue and his laughing eyes. Oh! Stinker.

I learned later that the man who had come to the door for Dad had seen a man swing a sack into the river. But he was too far away to be recognized except that he was very tall. My mind had sprung to Fitty Gunthorpe again, but when I put this to Dad he said, 'Aye, I thought that an' all and I went round there, but Fitty's been evacuated for the last month.'

I was deeply affected, not only by Stinker's death but by the way he had died, and day after day I cried about him until Dad, looking into my white face one morning, said firmly, 'Now look here, lass, he's gone and he can't be brought back and you've got the bairn to see to, so knuckle to.'

He was talking to the mother of Constance, but I did not feel a mother, I felt in this moment a very young girl who had lost her dog. Stinker hadn't only been a dog, he had been a person to whom in the darkness of the night I had whispered my thoughts, my pain.

All the time I had been carrying the child I had, in a way, been free, free from the pressure of both Ronnie and Don, but now the pressure was back, heavy and menacing. With Ronnie, it was his solicitude, for which at any moment he might ask payment or, what was more likely, plead for payment, for I had unheedingly broken down certain barriers for him: I was no longer a virgin, there was no question of being raped by my brother. With Don, it was the insidious penetration of himself into my life through the wall that separated us. For hours he would sing loudly and practise on a guitar, playing the one tune over and over again. And then every third week, when he was on the day shift, around twelve o'clock at night or at whatever time he returned from the bars, there would start a gentle tapping on the wall. This would last from ten minutes to anything up to an hour. The more tight he was the shorter would be the duration. I began to wait for the tapping, knowing it would come, for I could never go to sleep until it finished. It took swift payment of my nerves, for at times the soft tap-tap became loud in my head, like a hammer beating on tin, and I felt I must scream at him through the wall or go mad.

Between the two of them, I had good reason for asking Dad to change rooms again, but had I told him the situation I doubt whether he would have believed me. More likely he would have thought my mind was affected. I could not even make Constance the excuse for a change of room, for the child slept anywhere, and she never cried except when she was hungry, and then I had only to lift her from the cot where it was wedged between the wall and the foot of my bed.

And now I was back where I had started, with Don on one side and Ronnie on the other, the only difference being they were no longer boys, they were both men. Of the two, at this time, I think I was mostly afraid of our Ronnie, and this fear came to the surface one Friday night when, after placing his board money on the table, he pushed three pounds towards me, saying, 'Get yourself something.'

I looked at him, then turned sharply away from the light in his eyes, that soft, pleading light that could turn my stomach. I did not touch the money, but said, 'Thanks, but there's nothing I want.'

'Dont be silly,' he said; 'you're letting yourself go and you're not to do that. Get yourself a frock or something.' He picked the money up and put it on the mantelpiece.

I left the money where it was. And there it remained until Dad came in.

'Whose is this?' he asked, touching the notes.